WHERE THERE'S A WILL...

ALSO BY JOCKO WILLINK

WAY of the WARRIOR KID
FROM WIMPY TO WARRIOR THE NAVY SEAL WAY

WAY of the WARRIOR KID 2
Marc's Mission

WAY of the WARRIOR KID 4
FIELD MANUAL

WAY of the WARRIOR KID
THE COLORING BOOK!

MIKEY AND THE DRAGONS

WAY OF THE WARRIOR KID III

WHERE THERE'S A WILL...

JOCKO WILLINK

ILLUSTRATED BY **JON BOZAK**

JOCKO PUBLISHING

Way of the Warrior Kid III is published under Jocko Publishing, a sectionalized division in association with Di Angelo Publications INC.

JOCKO PUBLISHING
In association with Di Angelo Publications
4265 San Felipe #1100
Houston, Texas, 77027

Way of the Warrior Kid III Copyright 2019 Jocko Willink. Illustrated by Jon Bozak. In digital and print distribution in the United States of America.

www.jockopublishing.com
www.diangelopublications.com

Library of congress cataloging-in-publications data
Way of the Warrior Kid III. Downloadable via Kindle
Library of Congress Registration

Hardback

ISBN-10: 1-942549-48-2
ISBN-13: 978-1-942549-48-2

Facilitated by: Di Angelo Publications
Designed and illustrated by: Jon Bozak

First Edition

10 9 8 7 5 4 6 3 2 1

1. Children's fiction

2. Children's Fiction ——Narrative ——United States of America with int. Distribution.

This book is dedicated to
the courageous Frogmen of SEAL
Team Three, Task Unit Bruiser.
Especially, Marc, Mikey, Ryan, Chris, and Seth.
We will never forget them.

CHAPTER 1

Seventh grade has actually been pretty awesome. Until today. With only three days left before summer vacation, things took a turn for the worse.

I have stayed on the Warrior Kid Path for almost three years now. I'm stronger and faster and do better in school than most other kids. And I have some pretty good friends. Kenny Williamson, who used to be a bully, now hangs around with me a bunch. So does Nathan James, a kid that I used to think was super annoying. Now we are all good friends and they are all on The Path of being Warrior Kids. Nathan started jiu-jitsu with me last summer, and at the beginning of this school year, Kenny started training jiu-jitsu, too.

We have all kinds of fun all the time. And these guys pretty much looked up to me. I was like a leader, just like my Uncle Jake told me I would be. I like being a leader. And I felt like I was a leader—until today. Because today was the day when Danny Rhinehart arrived at my school. First of all, who shows up at school with only three days left? I get that he just moved here, but still, it's just silly! Why would someone do that? Anyway, he ended up coming into our homeroom with Mr. Oglethorpe.

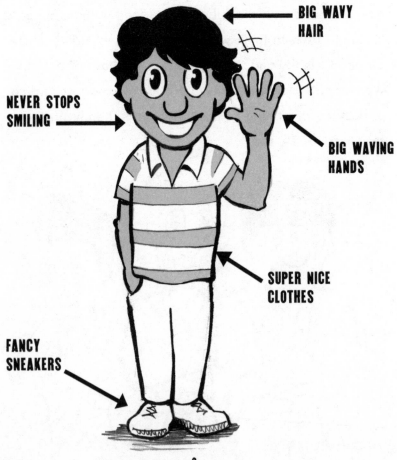

BIG WAVY HAIR

NEVER STOPS SMILING

BIG WAVING HANDS

SUPER NICE CLOTHES

FANCY SNEAKERS

Now, Danny seemed really nice when I first met him. He was all smiles and super polite to everyone. Maybe a little too nice! He was actually pretty tall, too—maybe a couple inches taller than me. He ended up getting put at our table because Jennifer Garston went with her parents to Minnesota for the summer and left school a few days early. And because he was only around for the last three days of school, Mr. Oglethorpe asked if Danny could just kind of stay with me for the day.

So, we finished homeroom and then went to math class. Because school was almost over, we were just doing some games in math. We had to see who could finish problems the quickest and who knew the most math facts. And even though Danny was new to the class, he did really well. REALLY WELL. He knew the answer to just about every question. His hand would shoot up every time the teacher asked any question at all.

Since Danny has all the answers, we might as well all go home...

And of course, the teacher would call on him—probably because he was the "new guy" and the teacher was trying to be nice. And the whole time Danny had this big smile on his face. A REALLY BIG SMILE. A smile so big that it was kind of ANNOYING.

Then we went out to recess. And Danny was with me. I figured it was time to see what Danny was really made of, so I took him over to the pull-up bar with Kenny and Nathan.

"We like to do pull-ups," I told Danny. "Get some, Kenny!"

With that, Kenny jumped up on the bar and knocked out fourteen straight pull-ups. That was pretty good and more than Kenny used to be able to do.

Then Nathan hopped up on the bar and he rattled off sixteen pull-ups in a row. That was impressive.

Finally, it was my turn. I was now pretty darn good at pull-ups. So I jumped up and knocked out a solid twenty-six pull-ups in a row. Not my best, but still decent—and a heck of a lot better than Nathan or Kenny.

"Nice!" Kenny shouted when I finished.

"Strong work, Marc!" Nathan added.

I would have done 27 but didn't want to show off.

I looked over at Danny. I thought he might be intimidated by all this, but he didn't look intimidated at all. Maybe that's because he didn't realize I was about to call him out and ask him to do pull-ups. I wanted him to see that even though he was good at math, there were other things in the world to be good at besides knowing math facts and how to figure out problems. Then he asked, "Do you mind if I have a go?"

That kind of surprised me. And he had a big smile on his face—like he was going to enjoy it. "Sure," I told him, "go ahead."

With that, Danny jumped up on the bar and immediately did a pull-up. Then another one. Then another one. And then another and another and another.

I was counting in my head. When he got to twenty, Nathan started counting out loud. "Twenty, twenty-one, twenty-two, twenty-three, twenty-four, twenty-five...twenty-six, twenty-seven–that's more than you, Marc!" Nathan shouted.

But Danny didn't stop. He kept going. And going. And finally got to thirty-two before he finally struggled on the last one, came up short, and then dropped off the bar.

"Thirty-two!" Kenny shouted. "That's a new record."

"Awesome work, Danny. Isn't that awesome, Marc?" Nathan added, looking at me.

I didn't really know what to say. I hadn't even done my maximum number. I could have done a few more, but I didn't. And now my friends thought Danny was 'AWESOME'.

"Yeah," I finally replied. "Awesome."

"It's no big deal," Danny said. "I had a pull-up bar at my old house, so I did them a bunch. I'm sure you could have done a few more if you had to."

SHEESH! Why would he even say something like that! He had clearly beaten me, and now he was saying it wasn't a big deal? Maybe he was just trying to make me feel worse by making it seem like it was no big deal.

"What kind of pull-up workouts do you do?" Nathan asked. But he wasn't asking me—he was asking Danny!

"Well, you know," Danny replied, "just basic stuff. I jump on the bar and do a bunch of pull-ups, then do that a bunch of times. It's nothing crazy."

Nothing crazy?!?! Here I had been working on pull-ups for three years and I still got beat! It was crazy. It was driving me crazy! That was when I realized that Danny was probably one of those people that was just naturally good at pull-ups. My Uncle Jake had told me about people like that—people that were just naturally good at something. So he probably didn't have to work hard at this at all—it was probably just easy for him.

But there were other things I was sure I could beat Danny at. At least I thought there would be.

CHAPTER 2

At the end of every school year, we have one day called
"field day". It is fun—at least it is now that I do better at
the events. I have even won some of them. This is a long
way from where I was in fifth grade when I couldn't
do a single pull-up. That was the summer that Uncle
Jake came and taught me how to work out, how to eat
healthy, how to study, how to swim, and even got me
started in jiu-jitsu so I wouldn't get bullied by Kenny Williamson, who became my friend after I stood up to him.

Last year I did pretty well at just about every event.
The only one I wasn't very good at was bobbing for
apples. I just couldn't get my mouth around the apple
because it wouldn't stay still in the water.

You'd think ONE would
at least stick to a tooth
or something.

But I did well in pull-ups, push-ups, sit-ups, burpees, and the one-mile run. In fact, I won all pull-ups, sit-ups, and burpees for my class. Tony Hale won the push-ups, I think because his arms are so short. And Iris beat me in the one mile run and won first place because she runs competitively and trains all the time! But field day was still a great time and I had a ton of fun.

This year was different. Very different. And I bet you can guess why. Danny Rhinehart. He won just about EV-ERYTHING. He beat me in pull-ups, sit-ups, and burpees. Tony still won push-ups, though. I did thirty-one pull-ups, Danny did thirty-seven. I did 107 sit-ups, Danny did 131. I did thirty-six burpees in two minutes, Danny did for-ty-two!

And every time he would win something, Danny would just act like it was no big deal. He would smile and shrug it off, like winning was so easy for him!

Wins come and go. No big deal...

But when it got to the mile run, I figured I could take him—and even win first place since Iris had broken her ankle in the spring and still wasn't allowed to run. So, since I got second last year, I figured with Iris out of the race, it was mine for the taking!

You couldn't beat me in a race if I had two broken ankles, Marc!

My class and Mr. Blackwell's class lined up for the race. The P.E. teacher, Mr. Sadolwski, then looked at us all and said, "On your mark, get set, GO!"

I sprang off the line and started to run hard. I wanted to get away from the rest of the kids and be out there on my own and away from the rest of the pack. In a race, the slower kids slowed me down if they were ahead of me. Not this time. I sprinted hard and got ahead of the pack. It didn't take long before I was in the lead, out in front of everyone, on my own.

Once out in front, I didn't even look back. Uncle Jake told me when racing, if you look around, you lose time and momentum, so I just kept charging ahead at a solid speed.

But being in first place wasn't enough—I wanted to make sure I not only beat Danny, but crushed him! So I ran really hard. Really hard!

Then, as I rounded one of the corners, I noticed some-one just a bit behind me. And of course, it was Danny! So I ran a little harder. It was a long straight away, so I just tried to run even harder, but I was already out of breath. I had to slow down just a little bit. But I thought I was far enough ahead of Danny to beat him.

As I slowed down, I kind of got my breath back, but I was still hurting.

Now, as I continued down the straightaway, I couldn't tell where Danny was without looking—and I needed to know. So, despite what Uncle Jake had taught me, I turned my head and looked behind me to see where Danny was. I saw him, and he WAS GAINING ON ME! That's right! Despite how hard I was running, Danny was running even faster.

I couldn't believe it! So I tried to pick up my pace a little more, but I just couldn't. My lungs were already burning!

But Danny wasn't slowing down. He was getting closer and closer to me. I could hear him breathing, and he was breathing HARD! Even harder than me.

I started to get mad! Mad that he was beating me—not just at this race, but at everything! So I decided I would try to run harder so I could stay ahead of him. We didn't have that much farther to go, so I stepped it up. But it wasn't enough. Moments later, Danny was right next to me. He was breathing like crazy. I looked at him from the corner of my eye, and he looked like he was going to die! If I could just hold on a little longer, I thought he might break!

But he didn't. He kept straining and breathing and fighting, and I just couldn't keep running so fast. My lungs just couldn't take it anymore. So I backed off. I let it go.

And as soon as I did, Danny pulled ahead of me. Not just by a little bit either. No! As I slowed down, he actually sped up and started running even *faster!*

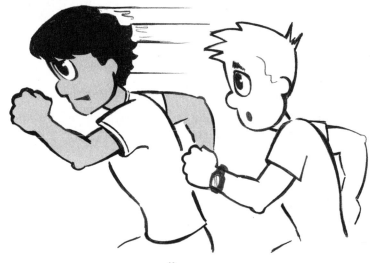

I couldn't believe it! Especially because there was no way I could run any harder. But Danny could.

So, I kept running, and I came in second place. When I got across the finish line, I looked for Danny, but I couldn't see him. Then I saw a crowd of people from the other classes looking at something. I walked over and saw Danny. He was lying on the ground, completely exhausted. I was tired, but not as tired as he was. And honestly, it felt pretty good seeing him there on the ground like that, because I knew he was way more tired than I was, which made me feel kind of like I had won.

But the crowd didn't think so. They were all telling him "great job" and "nice race". No one said anything to me.

When Nathan and Kenny finished the race, they asked if I had won.

"No. Danny Rhinehart won," I answered as I pointed to him lying on the ground, wanting them to see that he was more tired than I was. As soon as I said that, they ran over to see him—and to tell him he did a good job.

That feeling that I kind of won started slipping away, and I realized that Danny had beaten me again. And I didn't like it.

CHAPTER 3

On the last day of school, things got even worse with Danny. One of the last things we did in class was a game where we got tested on all the knowledge we had learned from every class. We got asked math problems, history questions, vocabulary, and some science. It seemed like it would be pretty fun. Here is how the game worked: Mr. Oglethorpe asked two people the same question, the first one to answer correctly stayed in the game and the other kid would be sent across the room to sit down on the floor—they were out of the game. Mr. Oglethorpe kept repeating that, leaving fewer and fewer people in the game.

Now, I thought I would do well at this game. I studied hard all year and paid attention during classes. I defi-

-nitely didn't think Danny would do very well, since he had been at a different school all year and would probably have learned different things than what we learned. Boy, was I WRONG.

It turns out Danny was really smart! He knew that the formula for volume was length times width times height. He knew the first amendment of the constitution protected free speech. He knew that an invertebrate was an animal without a spine. He knew what an acute angle and a repeating decimal were. I also knew the answers to the questions as well as the questions I got asked.

As the game pressed on, you guessed it, the last two people in the game were Danny Rhinehart and me!

The whole class was watching and cheering us on. Most of the kids were cheering for me because they knew me—and because Kenny and Nathan were cheering loudly for me!

When it was just the two of us left, Mr. Oglethorpe said, "Okay. For this final round, I will ask five questions. Whoever gets three of them right will be the champion. You guys got it?"

"Got it," I replied.

"Yes, sir," Danny said.

"Okay. First question is science. What is the function of mitochondria in a–"

"Mitochondria is the powerhouse of the cell!" I shouted. The class clapped for me. I knew this one for sure.

"That's right, Marc. Nicely done," Mr. Oglethorpe said.

Danny whispered, "Good job. You were fast," with a smile on his face. I thought he was just trying to psych me out.

"Okay, next question will be math," Mr. Oglethorpe said. "What is absolute val–"

"Absolute value is the distance between a number and zero," Danny exclaimed confidently.

"Oooooooooh," Nathan and Kenny and some of the class responded.

"That's right Danny. Nicely done. They taught you well at your last school. It is one to one. The next question will be about geography. What is the capital of Turkey?"

I wasn't a hundred percent sure on this one, but I could only remember one city in Turkey, so I took a shot. "Istanbul?"

"Nope. Not Istanbul," Mr. Oglethorpe said.

"Ankara?" Danny asked.

"Yes, it is, Danny! Nicely done. That is a tough question."

"Thanks Mr. Oglethorpe."

You're good, kid!

HOW DID HE KNOW THAT? I COULD BARELY EVEN RE-MEMBER ISTANBUL, WHICH IS THE MOST FAMOUS CITY IN TURKEY!

And that answer got some of the class cheering for Danny. I even saw that Kenny and Nathan were impressed with that answer.

Now the pressure was on.

"Okay, boys," Mr. Oglethorpe said, "it is now two to one with Danny in the lead. If he gets this one he wins. If you get it, Marc, there will be another question. Here we go. The next question is a math question. What is the name of a triangle where each side is a diff—"

"Scalene!" I shouted, "a triangle where each side is a different length is called a scalene triangle!" I knew it! The class cheered.

"That's right, Marc. Excellent! Two to two. All tied up," Mr. Oglethorpe said. The class clapped and hooted. "Okay, okay, quiet, quiet," Mr. Oglethorpe told the class, getting them to settle down. I looked at Danny. He was still smiling. I knew I wasn't. I wanted to win. I was focused. And there was Danny, with a big smile on his face! I didn't get it!

He's probably best friends with his dentist!

Finally, Mr. Oglethorpe spoke. "For the last question, we are going back to science. Ready?"

"I'm ready," I told him.

"Yes, sir," Danny said.

"Okay. What do you call a single-celled organism with no nucleus, no mitochondria, and no–"

"A prokaryote," Danny cut off Mr. Oglethorpe. "A prokaryote is a simple, single-celled organism that doesn't have a nucleus, no mitochondria, and no organelles."

I had no idea. I don't think anyone in the class knew either, because they all looked at Mr. Oglethorpe to see if Danny was right or not.

"That...is...CORRECT!" Mr. Oglethorpe said. The class cheered and Danny just sat there with a big smile on his face. Now even Nathan and Kenny were cheering. "We have a winner, our new student, Danny Rhinehart! Great work, Danny!"

And that was it. The class all stood up and we began talking. Kenny and Nathan came over to where Danny and I were standing.

"Nice work, guys," Nathan said.

"Yeah," Kenny added, "I don't know how you guys knew all that stuff!"

"Yeah. Parokry...pyrokar...what was that thing?" Nathan asked, unable to pronounce the word.

"Prokaryote," Danny said. "I got lucky on that one. I happened to remember a picture we had to memorize at my last school. It was hard for me to pronounce it, so I had to study it extra hard. I think that is why I remembered it."

Here was Danny, of course being all nice to everyone and saying he was just "lucky". For some reason, this just made me really mad.

So I said, "Well you wouldn't get so lucky on the jiu-jitsu mat."

Now Nathan and Kenny smiled. They knew that even though Danny might win a silly trivia contest, I could still tap him out on the mat!

"Jiu-jitsu?" Danny asked.

"Yes," I told him, "It's fighting. I've been training for three years."

I have jiu-jitsu moves so scary they even freighten me!

"Wow. That's awesome," Danny said with his typical big smile.

"Yes. It is awesome," I told him. It felt good knowing I could beat him on the mat.

Until he said, "I love jiu-jitsu. I have been training since I was eight! A little over four years! I have been wondering if there was a school here so I can go. What is the name of your school?"

I couldn't believe it! Danny beat me in pull-ups, then the run, then in the class quiz game, and now he trains jiu-jitsu and has even been training LONGER THAN ME! WHAT THE HECK?!?!?

"We train at Victory MMA. You should come," Nathan said.

"Yeah," Kenny added, "we have a great time there."

"Awesome. I will talk to my parents today. We can train all summer long," Danny said, still with his BIG SMILE.

I couldn't believe it. The final thing I thought I could beat Danny in—and it turned out he would probably be able to beat me. And now he was going to be training at my academy ALL SUMMER LONG. MY SUMMER WAS RUINED BEFORE IT HAD EVEN STARTED.

The good thing was that my Uncle Jake was coming. Maybe he could help.

CHAPTER 4

I was super excited when Uncle Jake arrived. But I was also nervous. I knew he expected me to be doing awesome in everything. After all, I have continued to live the Warrior Kid Code that I wrote after he taught me how to be a Warrior Kid.

It says:

1. The Warrior Kid wakes up early in the morning.
2. The Warrior Kid studies to learn and gain knowledge and asks questions if they don't understand.
3. The Warrior Kid trains hard, exercises, and eats right to be strong and fast and healthy.
4. The Warrior Kid trains to know how to fight so they can stand up to bullies to protect the weak.
5. The Warrior Kid treats people with respect and helps out other people whenever possible.
6. The Warrior Kid keeps things neat and is always prepared and ready for action.
7. The Warrior Kid stays humble and stays calm. Warrior Kids do not lose their tempers.
8. The Warrior Kid works hard, saves money, is frugal and doesn't waste things. The Warrior Kid always does their best.
9. I am the Warrior Kid and I am a leader.

When Uncle Jake finally arrived in a taxi from the airport, it was awesome to see him. He looked even stronger than ever!!

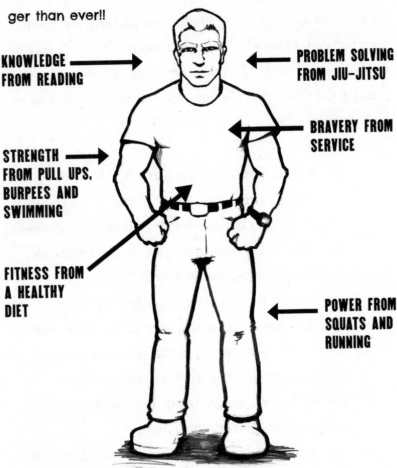

KNOWLEDGE FROM READING

PROBLEM SOLVING FROM JIU-JITSU

BRAVERY FROM SERVICE

STRENGTH FROM PULL UPS, BURPEES AND SWIMMING

FITNESS FROM A HEALTHY DIET

POWER FROM SQUATS AND RUNNING

As soon as I saw him I shook his hand and offered to take his bag up to my room, where he would be staying again.

"That's alright, Marc. I can handle it."

"You look like you are even bigger and stronger than before!" I said to Uncle Jake.

"Yeah. I have been working hard. Really hard. And eating healthy. So, I have been able to get in pretty good shape. But I still have a lot of work to do," Uncle Jake said. Then he asked, "What about you? How have you been doing?"

"Great. I am still staying on the path and living the Warrior Kid code. I studied hard in school all year long and got all "A's" on my report card. I still exercise almost every day. I eat healthy and barely ever eat junk food. So it's going pretty good. Of course, like you said, I have a lot of work to do, too!" I said with a smile, knowing that Uncle Jake would like my humility.

One of my best qualities is my humility.

"What about jiu-jitsu?" Uncle Jake asked.

"Yes, sir! I am still training hard all the time. And there is the big tournament at the end of the summer that I am going to compete in again this year."

"Sounds like everything is going great, Marc."

"It is!" I told him.

Then Uncle Jake got that serious look on his face he gets when he wants to teach me something important. "Okay. But you said you still had work to do. But what is it? If everything is going so great, what thing do you need help in?"

Of course, I didn't want to tell him about the whole situation with Danny Rhinehart. But I thought I could bring it up a little by talking about the one mile run, so I told him. "Running."

"Running?" Uncle Jake responded, surprised. "What is wrong with your running?"

"Well," I told him, "on field day at the end of the school year, we run a one-mile race. Last year I came in second to Iris Gardner. She runs cross country races all the time and is really good. But this year she couldn't run because she hurt her ankle. So I figured I would win."

Marc, If you don't stop using me as an excuse, I'm going to race you with my cast on!

"And?" Uncle Jake asked.

"And I didn't. There is this new kid in school named Danny Rhinehart, and he beat me. I was winning for a while, but then he pulled along side me and I just couldn't keep up. I felt like I was going to die."

"Danny Rhinehart, huh?"

"Yeah. I'm sorry Uncle Jake."

"No reason to be sorry. Let's see what we can learn from it. What was your time?"

"My time?"

"Yes. How long did it take you to run the mile?" Uncle Jake asked me.

"I'm not sure."

"You didn't time the race?" he asked, puzzled.

"No."

"Have you ever timed how fast you can run a mile?"

"No, Uncle Jake," I said. "We just run against each other. If you win, you win. If you don't, you don't."

"Well, if we are going to get you better at running, we need to figure out how fast you can actually run."

"Okay. But...." I wasn't sure that I should say what I was about to say, so I stopped myself. But Uncle Jake knew better.

"But what?" he asked.

"Well...." I was still unsure if I should say it.

"Well what?" Uncle Jake asked,

Now I knew I had to tell him. "Well, it's just that I don't really like running that much."

On a scale of 1 to 10 my running skills over around -100!

Uncle Jake was quiet for a moment. Then he looked at me and said, "I could have guessed that."

"Why?" I asked.

"Because you aren't comfortable when you run. It isn't easy. You have to push hard when you run, and that hurts. It hurts to be uncomfortable. And you don't like it. That's why you should do more of it."

"Wait. I tell you I don't like running, and you tell me I should do more of it?"

"Exactly. If there is something that you don't like doing, something that makes you uncomfortable, you should do more of it. It will make you better. And it will also make you more comfortable at being uncomfortable. So, let's go for a ride."

That's when Uncle Jake walked over and grabbed my mom's car keys. I followed him. We walked outside and got in the car. He started up the car and we headed out of the driveway. When we got to the end, he reset the odometer to zero, and we started driving. He drove down three blocks from my house and then took a left on the road that borders the park. That part of the road went up hill a bit, and at the top of the hill, there was a little wall about waist high at the gate outside the entry to the park.

"Perfect," Uncle Jake said.

"What's perfect?" I asked.

"From the driveway in front of your house to that little wall right there. That's a half mile. Slap the corner of that little wall with your hand and then hoof it back to your driveway. That's a mile. Got it?"

"Got it," I told Uncle Jake.

We drove back to the house and pulled into the driveway.

"Go get your running shoes. We are about to get you uncomfortable."

I went into the house and put on my running shoes. When I got back down, Uncle Jake was waiting with his shoes on.

"Ready?" Uncle Jake asked.

"I guess so," I told him.

"Being ready isn't a guessing game. Are you ready?"

That made sense. I was as ready now as I ever would be.

"Yes, Uncle Jake, I'm ready."

"Okay then," he said pressing some buttons on his watch. "When I say 'Bust 'em'" we go. Got it?"

"Got it, Uncle Jake."

"Standby...BUST 'EM!" Uncle Jake barked.

I took off running. I thought that Uncle Jake was going to take off ahead of me, but he didn't. He stayed right next to me.

"Pick up the pace," he said. I ran faster. We made it to the first block. I was running pretty fast.

"Go harder," Uncle Jake told me. "Step. It. Up." He was breathing hard, but not as hard as I was.

"I'm trying," I managed say between my breaths.

"TRY HARDER," he replied sternly.

By the time we got to the third block, I was really hurting.

"Push through it, Marc. You have to push through it," Uncle Jake told me. "You have to push through that pain."

"I...am," I whispered through gasping breath.

"No, you aren't." And with that Uncle Jake took off ahead of me. He sprinted around the left corner and took off up the hill. When he got to the top, he slapped the corner of the wall and sprinted back down past me on the way back home.

He didn't say anything as he went past me. He just ran.

I kept going up the hill, slapped the corner of the wall, and then made my way back home. With Uncle Jake out of my ear, I slowed down a little bit.

Finally, I got within sight of my driveway. Uncle Jake started yelling at me. "Finish strong! With everything you've got!" I ran a little faster and made it to my house.

"Seven-o-nine," Uncle Jake said.

"What?" I asked him.

"Seven minutes and nine seconds. That was your time."

"Oh. Okay."

Uncle Jake let me catch my breath a bit. Then he said, "Not okay. You don't know how to really push yourself yet."

"I pushed myself!" I protested. I was wondering how he could say that when I was standing there breathing so hard.

"Yes. You pushed yourself. But you didn't really push yourself. It's okay. You'll learn, Marc. You'll learn."

With that, Uncle Jake walked back toward the house and I stood out there in the driveway, wondering what it was I had to learn.

CHAPTER 5

Well, today was TERRIBLE. Summer started and I went to jiu-jitsu class today. I was looking forward to it. Since I had been training for almost three years, I was one of the better kids at my jiu-jitsu academy, Victory MMA.

Plus, since I was one of the better kids, Coach Adam had me help out with classes, meaning I was like a junior instructor. On top of that, Nathan and I still helped clean the academy so that Nathan could train there for a little lower cost, and Kenny usually helps us out too because, well, I guess he doesn't have anything better to do.

So with everything that I did at the academy and as much time as I spent there and with my friends being there, Victory MMA was like my second home. I loved being there.

And I have to admit, being one of the best students there also made it fun. I was sort of a leader there and I could feel that the other kids looked up to me a little bit. That felt pretty good.

But today didn't feel good. AT ALL.

When I showed up, guess who was already there, wearing his gi? Yep, DANNY RHINEHART! And he was a yellow belt with four stripes—meaning he was almost an orange belt. That's the way it worked.

I'm beginning to think this kid has super powers!

You started off as a white belt and got stripes, or degrees, put on it. Once you had four stripes on your white belt, the next belt was gray. When you trained hard and learned new moves, you got stripes on the gray belt. Once you got four stripes on your gray belt, the next level was yellow belt, which was what I had. But I had only just gotten it and didn't have any stripes yet. And there was Danny with four stripes.

But the stripes and the belts didn't mean everything. In fact, Coach Adam always told us not to worry about what color your belt was or how many stripes you had. Uncle Jake said the same thing. What matters is how hard you trained and how well you could do the techniques. And just because someone had a higher belt didn't mean they could beat you. There were times when lower belts beat higher belts. It didn't usually happen, but it did sometimes happen. I was hoping it would happen with Danny!

I'm not saying I want to be the kid that beats Danny, but I am saying that I don't want to be the kid that doesn't beat him!

"Hi, Marc!" Danny said with a big smile on his face. He was always smiling and being so nice. For some reason, it was really kind of annoying.

"Hey, Danny," I said back to him. I don't think I was smiling though.

"Thanks for inviting me to your academy. This place is awesome!" he said.

I didn't invite you, I was thinking. At that point, Coach Adam walked over.

"Hey, buddy, how're you doing? I'm Coach Adam. Where you coming in from? It looks like you have trained before," Coach Adam said, as he pointed at Danny's belt.

"Yes, sir. I just moved here. But I have trained jiu-jitsu for about four years. Ever since I was eight."

"That's great. Did you meet Marc here?" Coach Adam asked, pointing over to me. I started to nod and say yes, but Danny cut me off.

"Yes, sir, we have met," Danny said. "We met at school and he invited me to come and train here. I really appreciate it."

"Well, it's great to have you. We can use all the good people we can get. The better students we have here, the better everyone can get. You guys can go spar while we are waiting for class to start."

"Great!" exclaimed Danny.

Oh no, I thought to myself. *This is horrible.* If we went through class together, I might not have to spar against Danny. And even if we did end up sparing, it would be at the end of class and the rounds would be short and I would at least get to see what kind of skills he had during class and figure out how I could beat him. But that wasn't happening.

It's not like I had a great plan for beating Danny anyway...

"Okay," I said as we walked over the mat.

We took off our shoes and walked on the mat. Just as we did, Nathan and Kenny came through the door and walked right over to us. They didn't even have on their gis. They just took off their shoes and walked right onto the mat.

"Are you guys gonna go?" Nathan asked.

"Yeah," I told Nathan.

"Awesome," Kenny said.

I could feel myself getting tense, but Danny looked completely relaxed. We shook hands, bowed, and then started.

Danny reached for the collar of my gi. I batted his hand away. He reached for it again. I batted it away again. He reached for it a third time. As I tried to bat it away again, he grabbed it with his other hand and flung me to the ground while he slipped behind me with a wrestling move called an arm drag and then hooked my leg and forced me down to the mat.

"Nice takedown!" Nathan said.

Danny was good. REALLY GOOD. Before I could even think about what was happening, Danny had moved into the mount position—one of the best places for him to be—and one of the worst places for me to be. This meant

Danny was on top of me with all his weight in a good position to TAP ME OUT! I couldn't believe it!

But Danny got a little too excited. He reached his arms around my neck and prepared to choke me, but I grabbed ahold of his right arm, trapped his right leg, and rolled him over so I was back on top, inside Danny's guard.

That meant I was between his legs, which gave him some control over my bodyweight. But I had escaped his mount and was now on top!

"Nice escape, Marc!" Nathan yelled.

I felt better and was glad that I had regained control. I looked at Kenny and Nathan who were sitting on the side of the mat watching closely. Coach Adam had walked over, too, so he could check out how well I would do against this higher belt. I felt good. I gave them a little nod to let them know I had this situation under control and I was about to do some moves that would crush Danny.

Just as I gave them that nod, I felt a fast movement in Danny's hips. He quickly slid them out to the side and put one of his legs over my arm and extended his hip as he held on to my arm. I knew exactly what he was doing: an armlock from the guard. But it was too late. I didn't react in time. Before I could even make a defensive move, my arm was fully straightened out and I had to tap. It was over. I couldn't believe it.

"Whoa! ARMLOCK!" Nathan shouted.

I already knew that, NATHAN! I thought to myself.

Dear arm, how could you let that armlock happen? You're supposed to be the arm expert!

"I guess I got kind of lucky with that," Danny said.

"I guess," I said back to him, not even knowing what to say.

"Nice move," Coach Adam said to Danny. "That was a solid armlock. You have some impressive skills, Danny. Now, you guys take a break. Nathan and Kenny, sweep up the mats and let's get ready for class."

Danny has impressive skills, I repeated in my head. I ALREADY KNEW THAT!

Was there anything Danny didn't have?

I couldn't think of anything Danny couldn't do.

Or anything that I liked about him. No. I didn't like him at all.

CHAPTER 6

Only a few days into summer and it already stunk.

I always thought summer was supposed to be relaxing! But for me, it wasn't at all. And now the one thing I enjoyed the most, jiu-jitsu, had become miserable.

On top of that, my business, Marc's Meticulous Mowing, had grown. Sure, it used to be fun to mow a couple of lawns during the summer and make some extra money. But now it was just getting crazy. I was mowing lawns, pulling weeds, clearing brush, and doing all kinds of work for people every day.

MY NEW LOGO FOR MARC'S METICULOUS MOWING!

It's not easy being the most popular, jiu-jitsu-practicing, lawn mowing kid in town!

And today I was at jiu-jitsu again, and of course Danny was there AGAIN. I was telling Nathan and Kenny about all the work I did, and Danny was sitting there listening.

He had a funny look on his face. Like he was surprised I worked so much.

So I said to him, "What about you, Danny? What do you do besides jiu-jitsu every day?"

"Well," Danny said, "I spend most of my time hanging out with my older brother Anthony."

"How old is he?"

"He's fourteen, just a couple years older than me. We do a lot of cool stuff."

"Does he train jiu-jitsu?" Nathan asked.

"Nah, jiu-jitsu really isn't his thing," Danny replied. "We mostly just hang around the house and do fun stuff."

It was exactly as I had figured. While I work hard every single day, Danny is just sitting around the house doing fun stuff with his brother. No wonder he is so good at jiu-jitsu!

When I got home, I talked to Uncle Jake about all of this. "I like having a business and I like making money, but I think it is just too much right now."

"Why do you think that?" Uncle Jake asked.

"It's all I do! I have work to do every day. There is just too much. It would be nice if it didn't take up all my time," I told him.

"But your business is doing well. You will be able to make a lot of money this summer."

"I know, Uncle Jake. And that's great. I want to train jiu-jitsu more and maybe hang around with my friends a little," I responded. I didn't think Uncle Jake was going to like this. He wasn't much of a fan of 'hanging around'.

Uncle Jake looked at me for a minute, then said, "What if you could do both those things?"

"Both what things?" I asked, not sure what he was talking about.

"Work and hang out with your friends."

"I guess that would be cool," I answered back, wondering where he was going with this. "But how can I do that?"

"Well," Uncle Jake said, "let's look at your situation. You have a lot of work to do. It takes up most of your time. And you want to spend more time with your friends. I think there is a way to make both those things happen."

"How?" I asked.

"I think it is time you got some employees."

"Employees? You mean hire people to help me?" That seemed like a crazy idea. Who would want to work for a kid?!?!?

"Yes."

Uncle Jake didn't seem to see what was so unclear to me, so I asked him, "Uncle Jake, who on earth would want to work for a kid?"

"Really?" Uncle Jake asked. "You can't figure this out?"

I had no idea what he was talking about. So I stood there with a blank look on my face.

"You don't think your friends might want to earn some money, too?"

Finally, it hit me! Kenny and Nathan! They could help me!

I spy two future employees of the month...

FOR HIRE!

FOR HIRE!

When I got a big smile on my face, Uncle Jake realized I had figured it out.

"Right?" he said, knowing that his idea was brilliant.

"Yes, Uncle Jake!" I told him. "I can get Kenny and Nathan to help me. They can make money, we can get the work done quicker and have more time to hang out!"

"That's it," Uncle Jake said.

The next day I got to jiu-jitsu and made the offer to Nathan and Kenny. "Do you guys want some money?"

Nathan looked at me like I was crazy. "Money? Do we want money?" he asked.

"Of course we want money!" Kenny said

"DUH!" Nathan added.

"Well that's awesome. Because if you want it, then you can get it," I told them.

All the cool kids wanna be my friend!

"We just said we wanted it!" Nathan said loudly.

"Okay, okay," I told them, "but you are going to have to work for it."

"Work for it? How? We're too young to work," Kenny protested.

"No, you aren't. You just haven't applied to the right companies," I told them both.

"I haven't applied to any companies!" Nathan said, laughing out loud.

"That's right. But I happen to know a company that is growing quickly and needs people with your skills."

"Our skills? Really? I'm not quite sure if I have any skills at all," Kenny said.

"Well, you both have the skill of being able to do manual labor," I said.

"Manual labor? I don't even know what that is!" said Nathan, still laughing from his last joke.

I laughed too, and finally got it together to say, "Manual labor means hard work. The company I know of needs two manual laborers. People willing to do hard work. But you will get paid for your hard work."

"Okay. I don't mind working hard. What is the name of the company?" Kenny asked.

"It's called Marc's Meticulous Mowing and Lawn Care!" I said with a big smile on my face.

"Wait, your company? Your lawn mowing company?" Nathan asked.

"It's really become more than just lawn mowing, I do all—"

"Yes!" Nathan cut me off.

"What?" I asked him.

"Yes! I'll take the job! Hire me!" Nathan shouted. "I'm IN!"

"Me too!" added Kenny.

"Great!" I shouted. "We can start tomorrow morning. My house at 8:00, after I get done working out."

"I'll be there!" Nathan said.

"Me too," said Kenny.

And just that quickly, I had a whole new attitude about my business. Instead of dreading work the next day, I was actually looking forward to it.

Looked like Uncle Jake was right again.

CHAPTER 7

The next morning I got up early and did a great work-out with Uncle Jake. We did pull-ups, push-ups, sit-ups, squats, and burpees. It was tiring! But I didn't even have time to be tired. As soon as I got done, I had to get ready to work.

Yep, my business, Marc's Meticulous Mowing and Lawn Care, was doing great. I had a ton of work to do. During the winter, I only worked on the weekends, but as soon as summer came along and grass and weeds started growing, a lot of the neighborhood had work for me to do.

Right at 8:00, Nathan and Kenny showed up—and they were ready to work! We loaded the tools into my wagon and headed over to the Kurth's house.

I explained to them what we had to do. I was going to be in charge of mowing the lawn; as I was doing that, they would both pull weeds. As soon as I was done

with the mowing, I would use the weed-whacker while
they were raking up the lawn.

Once I was done with
the weed-whacking, we
would sweep and clean,
and that would be it.

We went to work and it
was awesome. Nathan and
Kenny worked hard and we
got the job done fast!

Then we moved to the
McDermott's house, then the
Washington's house, then
the O'Brien's, and finally the
Madison's. It took a while,
but it was still moving A LOT
faster than it did when I had
to do it alone.

I could see that Nathan and Kenny were starting to
slow down.

"You do this every day?" Nathan asked me.

"Yep. Pretty much," I replied. "But with your help, at least we can finish early and have some time to relax before jiu-jitsu."

"That'll be good."

We finally finished the last house, loaded up the wagon and headed back to my house. When we got there, we put the tools away.

"Well, I'm going to go get something to eat," Kenny said.

"Me too," Nathan added.

"Okay. Wait one second." I reached into my pocket and pulled out eighteen dollars. "Nine for you and nine for you," I said as I handed them nine dollars each.

"Really?" Nathan asked.

"Yep. You guys really helped me out today and I appreciate it. Now, who wants to work again tomorrow?"

"Me!" Nathan shouted.

"Me too!" added Kenny.

"Awesome. Well, I'll see you guys at jiu-jitsu tonight."

After they both left, I went inside and sat down on the couch. I was feeling tired, but boy was it nice to have some time to relax. I was also hungry, so I got up and walked toward the kitchen. Uncle Jake was sitting at the dining table doing some work.

How was it?

"How was it?" he asked.

"It was great. They both worked really hard. We had fun and got the job done in less than half the time."

"That's great. And it leaves you some time for your run," Uncle Jake said.

This caught me a little off guard. I had finished work early. I was going to make some food and relax for a while.

"Well, actually, Uncle Jake, I was just going to grab some food and...."

"You should eat after the run, so your stomach doesn't bother you," Uncle Jake cut me off.

"I know that, but I was not actually planning on running. I already worked out today and I just did a bunch of yard work and I have jiu-jitsu tonight so I was just going to, you know, relax a little."

Uncle Jake sat and looked at me. Finally, he said, "Oh. I thought you wanted to get better at running."

This was one of Uncle Jake's little tricks, and I knew it. He knew it too.

For my next trick I will make you stronger, faster and wiser...

But it was working. "I do want to get better at running, Uncle Jake, but...."

"But nothing," he said, cutting me off. "'Relaxing' does not make you better at running. Running does. Now go get your shorts on for a run."

He was right. I knew it. I went and put my shorts on

and then headed to the front of the house where Uncle Jake was waiting.

"Let's see you pick up the pace today," he said. "Okay?"

"Okay, Uncle Jake," I told him.

"Alright, then. Standby...BUST 'EM!"

I took off running and Uncle Jake was right with me.

He held a little bit faster pace than me, and I tried to keep up.

"Let's go. Step it up!" Uncle Jake said. I tried for a while. But then it started to hurt a little too much, and I just couldn't keep going. I slowed down.

"Don't let up!" Uncle Jake said, turning his head over his shoulder and looking at me. "Stay with me."

"I'm trying...." I panted.

"No, you're not," Uncle Jake said. Then he looked ahead and picked up the pace, pulling even farther ahead of me. He didn't look back again. He got to the corner, turned around and passed me as he headed home. He was running as fast as I could even imagine a person running–it was like an all-out sprint! And he didn't even look at me. He just looked ahead, and his face looked like he was in pain that he was just holding back–it was actually scary to see.

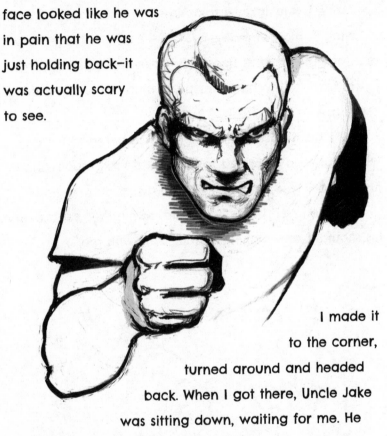

I made it to the corner, turned around and headed back. When I got there, Uncle Jake was sitting down, waiting for me. He looked at me and asked, "How was it?"

"Not bad. I think I improved my time a little bit. So at least I'm moving in the right direction."

"Why can you talk?"

"What?"

"You're talking. Why is that?" Uncle Jake asked, looking mad.

"Well, because you asked me a question, Uncle Jake," I responded nervously.

"That's not what I mean. You're talking because you didn't go hard. If you went hard, you wouldn't even be able to talk when you finished. You stayed in your comfort zone."

"My what?" I asked Uncle Jake.

"Your comfort zone," he said sharply. "That's where you ran. Where you were comfortable. Where you could handle it. Where you weren't breathing too hard and there wasn't much pain. That nice little place where everything feels just fine. That's how you ran and that's how you always run. That's the comfort zone. And that's why you aren't running fast. Because it hurts to run hard."

NOT the zone I need to be in!

57

This didn't make any sense to me. Why would Uncle Jake want me to get hurt? "But, Uncle Jake, I don't want to get hurt."

"Not that kind of hurt. Not an injury. A good kind of hurt. A good kind of pain. The pain that means you are getting out of your comfort zone—pushing yourself. And that is a good thing. Because if you stay in your comfort zone, you'll never get better. Does that make sense?"

"Yes, it does, Uncle Jake. I can try harder," I told him.

"Good," he said. "Because today you ran that mile in seven minutes and eight seconds. Next time, I want it done in under seven. And you won't be able to do that unless you push harder and get out of your soft little comfort zone. Got it?"

"Yes, Uncle Jake, I got it."

Uncle Jake walked away and, for the first time in a long time, I felt like I had let Uncle Jake down. I didn't want to let it happen again.

CHAPTER 8

Today started off really bad in jiu-jitsu, but it ended up REALLY GOOD.

Sometimes when we trained, we trained without the gi, which is the jiu-jitsu uniform. Sometimes we trained with it. Both ways are fun. Lately we had been wearing our uniforms more for training, because the tournament at the end of the summer was with the gi. Today we were training with the gi, and at first it was not fun at all because Danny was destroying me.

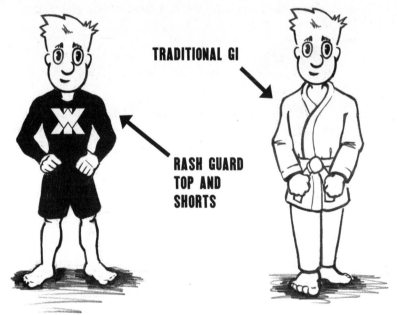

TRADITIONAL GI

RASH GUARD
TOP AND
SHORTS

He was fast and strong—but he was also really good at jiu-jitsu. He usually knew the defense to every move that I tried on him, how to do it, and he knew the de-

-fense really well. When he started doing moves on me, it was a real problem. He always made me think he was going to do one thing and then did something else. When he did get a move on me, he was so strong that it was hard to escape.

So Danny was all over me. I was rolling the best I could, but he was always a little bit ahead of me. When I tried to pass his guard, he swept me and ended up on top. Then, as I tried to sweep him, he passed my guard. As I tried to replace my guard, he mounted me. From there, he started to choke me and as I defended the choke, BOOM, he put an arm lock on me and made me tap out.

Arm, we talked about this...

"That worked better than I thought it would," he said *BETTER THAN YOU THOUGHT IT WOULD? REALLY?* I thought to myself. Danny always acts like everything is luck or like he really isn't that good—which I don't like one bit, because that means I AM EVEN WORSE!

"Let's go again," I said, determined to do better.

"Sure," Danny said with a smile...that smile that AN-NOYED ME LIKE CRAZY!

We shook hands and started again. This time, I shot in for the take down and got it. I put Danny on his back, but I ended up in between his legs in his guard. From there, I looked to get around his legs so I could do a submission on him. But before I could really make any progress, he sat up, lifted his hips, and sent me sailing through the air back onto the bottom position with him mounted on me AGAIN. This time when he went for the choke, I was more careful with my arms. TOO CAREFUL. By the time I actually tried to defend the choke, it was too late and I needed to tap AGAIN.

"That choke works well," Danny said to me.

I KNOW IT DOES, I thought to myself. I was getting frustrated, so I took a breath to calm down. I knew I could do better. And I thought of an idea: my secret move, called the 'loop choke'.

"Let's go one more time," I told Danny.

"That'd be great!" Danny said, still smiling. Of course he was smiling! He was crushing me!

We shook hands and started again.

I made Danny work hard, but I kind of let him take me down. Then he was in my guard. I grabbed his gi collar by his neck, loosely, so he wouldn't suspect anything. You see, in jiu-jitsu, there are a lot of moves that you can do where you actually use the gi against your opponent. There are ways of grabbing the gi that help you take your opponent down, trap their arm, or even choke them. The loop choke I was about to use on Danny used his gi against him. But I didn't want him to know the choke was coming, so I didn't grab the gi very tightly at all.

Then I let Danny start to pass my guard, which means get around my legs. To do that, he sunk his head down on my chest, but he didn't notice that I had snuck his gi under his chin and onto his neck.

Then, just as he started to get around me, I reached up around his head with my other hand, grabbed my own sleeve and squeezed—this was the loop choke—I had his neck caught in the loop of his own gi and I was closing the loop.

It was tight! I felt Danny start to get tense—he hadn't seen the choke coming. He tried to pull away, but couldn't because I was holding him behind the head. He tried to drive forward, but that only made the choke tighter. Then I felt him panic. His body jerked around and he put one of his hands up by my face as he tried to push me away. It did no good. This choke was TIGHT.

He struggled a little more but I held on—and then suddenly, he had enough and he tapped—hard and fast! I GOT HIM!

I let go and Danny looked up at me. I didn't know what he was going to say. I had finally beaten him!

"That was awesome!" Danny said with a big smile.

"Thanks," I said, surprised at his reaction.

Wait, so you're glad I beat you?

"What move was that? How did you do it?" he immediately asked.

That caught me off guard. That meant that he had
no idea what I had just done. He didn't even know what
the move was called! And obviously, he didn't know
what the defense was either. Then I paused and thought
to myself that if he didn't know what it was, I would be
able to keep getting him in it. Eventually he would be
able to figure it out, but for now, I thought I might as
well keep my secret move a secret!

"I'm not really sure. I just kind of grabbed onto your
neck and squeezed."

"Wow. Well, it worked great—whatever it was," Danny
said.

"Thanks." When I looked over, I saw Coach, who had
been watching the whole thing. Luckily, he hadn't heard
what I told Danny, so my secret was safe. And I'm sure
Coach was proud that I was able to beat him.

"Bring it in everyone," Coach Adam said to the class.
We all gathered around him in the center of the mat.
"Listen," he said in a serious tone, "we have the big tournament at the end of summer. And we have a lot of kids
that will be competing. I will have a lot of work to do as
we train to get ready and a lot of work the day of the
tournament. I need some help. So I am going to pick a
team captain to help me out."

That was AWESOME, I thought to myself. *I might be a TEAM CAPTAIN!*

"The team captain will help run practice, help keep track of equipment, and help warm everyone up at the tournament. I will pick the captain not just because of jiu-jitsu skills, but also because of attitude and leadership. I will choose a person who is a team player. Any questions?" Coach Adam asked.

No one said anything. But I was excited.

"Okay then, bring it in," Coach said. We all circled up close and put a hand in the middle of the circle. "Victory on three!" Coach shouted, "one, two, three..."

"Victory!" we all yelled.

Victory was our gym. And I was aiming to be its captain.

CHAPTER 9

I woke up this morning and Uncle Jake met me down in the garage for our workout.

"Just do five pull ups, Marc," he told me. This was a small number, so I was a little surprised. I did them.

"Now ten squats," he said.

"Got it," I replied and started doing squats.

"Ten push-ups when you are done."

"Okay," I said, surprised that this workout was kind of easy so far. I finished the push-ups.

"Okay, now do it again—five pull-ups, ten squats, ten push-ups. Nice and slow, I just want you to stretch out a bit."

I followed Uncle Jake's instructions and completed another round.

"One more time through," he told me.

"On it," I responded, and knocked out another set of pull-ups, squats, and push-ups. This was weird. This was much easier than our normal workouts.

"Now just stretch out a bit," Uncle Jake told me.

"Okay." I did some stretches with my shoulders and neck.

"Stretch the legs more," Uncle Jake said. This made me think. He must have some leg exercises coming my way. I reached down and grabbed my toes and stretched out my hamstrings, the muscles on the back of the leg above the knee.

After another couple of minutes of stretching, Uncle Jake looked at me. "You good?"

"Good for what?" I asked him.

"Are you ready?"

"Ready for what?" I asked, not quite sure what I was supposed to be getting ready for.

"Doesn't matter. ARE YOU READY OR NOT?" Uncle Jake questioned me with a stern voice, which told me I just needed to be ready, NOW!

"Yes, Uncle Jake. I'm ready."

"Good," he said, "because you are going to go run a mile, and you are GOING TO get out of your comfort zone and you are GOING TO run the mile in less than seven minutes. Understand?"

You couldn't do a 7-minute mile with a race car!

"Yes, Uncle Jake. I understand. I'll do my best."

"No. Not today. Your best hasn't been good enough. You need to dig deeper. You need to go harder. You need to get out of your comfort zone and run with everything you've got. DO YOU UNDERSTAND?" Uncle Jake actually seemed mad at me. I knew I was going to have to run HARD!

"Yes, Uncle Jake. I understand."

"Good," he replied, "let's go," and he walked out the door. I followed him as he made his way down the driveway. We lined up in position to start.

"Alright. I need you to run HARD. As hard as you can. Okay?"

"Okay."

"Here we go. Standby...

BUST
EM!

I took off running, Uncle Jake was right behind me. I was running at a hard pace. REALLY HARD. A pace I knew I couldn't keep up—but I was going to try.

By the end of the second block, I was already breathing hard.

"Stay with me," Uncle Jake said. "STAY WITH ME."

I was trying, but about halfway through the third block, my lungs were starting to BURN! I could feel fire in my throat!

I backed off a little bit—and as soon as I did, Uncle Jake knew somehow.

"KEEP THE PACE. YOU NEED TO PUSH THROUGH THE PAIN."

I couldn't answer because I was breathing too hard. But I did pick up the pace and was running full-throttle and staying with Uncle Jake.

"Now, when we turn the corner and start heading up the hill, this is what we are going to do: GO FASTER."

I didn't answer, but Uncle Jake must have seen the look on my face, which was questioning how I could possibly run FASTER.

"Don't look like that," Uncle Jake said. "Don't feel sorry for yourself. Put those feelings out of your mind and just do it. RUN HARDER. Stop thinking and do."

I listened to Uncle Jake. And I did what he told me to do. I stopped thinking about the pain, stopped feeling sorry for myself and just RAN. AS HARD AS I COULD.

When we turned the corner and headed up the hill, I RAN EVEN HARDER.

I felt the burning in my lungs and the soreness in my legs—I ignored them and ran harder.

And then the pain and the burning faded, and my mind was empty other than a voice inside saying, *run harder, run harder.*

When we got to the top of the hill, I tagged the fence-post and turned around.

For a split second, I hesitated. Reaching the half-way point at the fence felt good, and I was proud of how fast I had run it. As my mind drifted and relaxed for a moment, I was snapped out of it by Uncle Jake.

"GO. NO MERCY!" he yelled.

No mercy? Sheesh. I had never heard Uncle Jake say that before! And it got me FIRED UP. He took off down the hill in a full sprint and I followed him—as FAST AS I COULD.

I felt great going down the hill. But when I got to the bottom, it hit me.

The motivation from Uncle Jake's "No mercy" comment faded.

I suddenly felt the pain in my legs and the burning in my lungs again.

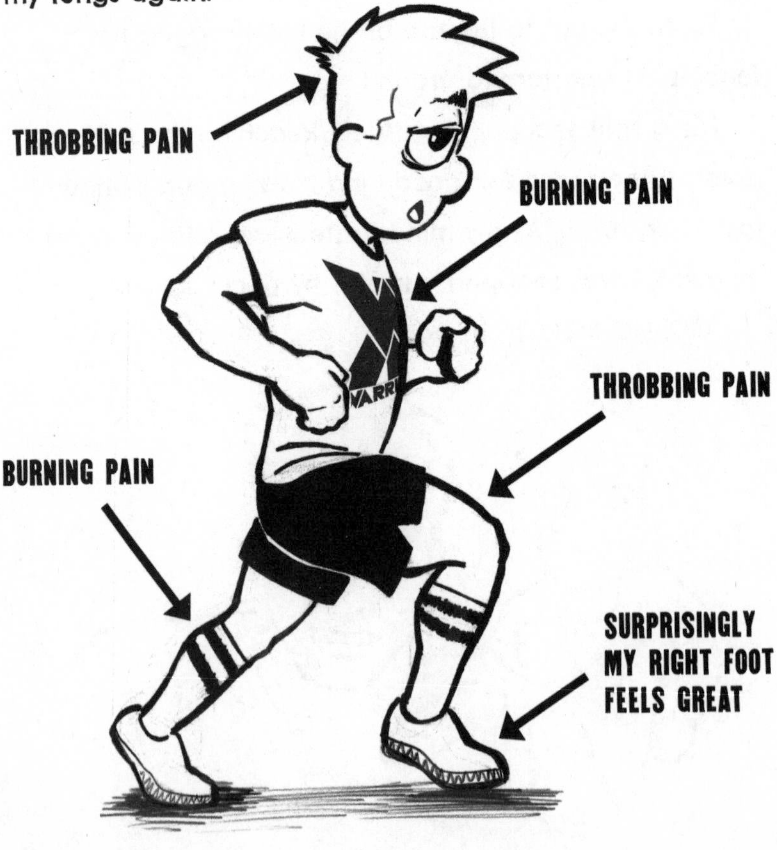

THROBBING PAIN

BURNING PAIN

THROBBING PAIN

BURNING PAIN

SURPRISINGLY MY RIGHT FOOT FEELS GREAT

I backed off. I slowed down. Just a little bit, and just for a second. And as soon as I did, again it seemed like Uncle Jake knew it. He looked back over his shoulder, saw me, and slowed down.

"There it is. You just went back into your comfort zone."

I kept running. I wasn't comfortable, but I wasn't pushing myself as hard as I had been.

"You have to push through it, Marc. You have to. I know you're tired. I know your lungs are screaming. It doesn't matter. IT DOESN'T MATTER. STEP IT OUT. WE ARE ALMOST THERE. STEP. IT. OUT!"

I didn't want to run harder, but more importantly, I didn't want to let Uncle Jake down.

I dug deep, put aside the pain and the agony I was feeling in my legs and lungs, and ran as hard as I could.

By the time I got to the last block, I didn't think I had anything left. BUT I DID. I ran as hard as I could all the way to the finish line at my driveway. As soon as I got across it, I stopped and collapsed to the ground.

I'm just going to take a little break for a minute or fifty...

"Stand up, hands up!" Uncle Jake said. I didn't move a muscle.

"Stand up, hands up," he said again.

I looked at him. He was standing there with his hands over his head like he had just won a race.

"Come on. GET UP," he said one last time.

I pushed myself back to my feet. I was exhausted.

"Hands up," Uncle Jake said again as he raised his hands over his head. "Get 'em up."

I put my hands up over my head. It did feel pretty good.

"Six forty-eight. You did it."

"What?" I asked, too tired to even know what Uncle Jake was talking about.

"Six minutes and forty-eight seconds. You just ran a mile in under seven minutes. Good work."

"Yes!" I shouted as I got my breathing under control.

"But more important," Uncle Jake said, "you got out of your comfort zone. That's what I like."

"Thanks, Uncle Jake," I said.

And it was kind of weird. Because even though it didn't feel good to get out of my comfort zone because it hurt, at the same time, it really did feel good to get out of my comfort zone because I knew I was getting better. I needed to remember that. Always.

CHAPTER 10

I DON'T LIKE DANNY RHINEHART.

I don't like his smile, I don't like his voice, I don't like the fact that he is so smart and so fast and so good at jiu-jitsu. I don't like his face. I DON'T LIKE HIM.

And today made that perfectly clear. We had to train together again today. I was hoping to get him in another loop choke, so I didn't mind too much when he took me down. I immediately grabbed the collar of his gi again and began setting up the choke. He leaned into me and started to pass my guard. I was just about to reach with my other hand to catch him in the choke when he swam his head under my arm and got his neck completely free. That was okay, because he was thrown off balance. I grabbed his arm that was bracing him from falling over and swept him so now I was on top.

It was a great sweep, but Danny managed to get me in his guard. So I started to work on getting past his guard. But that wasn't easy with Danny. He was strong and really good at messing with my balance. He pulled me in, pushed me back, pulled me in, then pushed me back again. I had no control.

Then he almost swept me but I stuck out my arm to stop from falling over. When I did that, he made some really strange movements. His hips moved, then he grabbed my head and pushed it; then he scooted to the side while reaching for the belt on my gi. I had no idea what was happening.

Then, all of a sudden, I was curled up in a ball with

one arm intertwined with Danny's legs. That would have been bad, but things got worse. Danny moved in more strange ways, but I could barely move at all. I didn't get it until I felt pressure increasing on my shoulder. I tried to resist, but I couldn't. Danny's legs were wrapped tight around my arm and I was stuck.

I didn't want to tap to this because it didn't even seem like a real move! Danny slowly shifted his weight further and further forward, twisting my shoulder more. I tried one more time to get my arm out of this lock, but it wouldn't budge. But I didn't want to tap!

So instead of tapping, I yelled, "Ahhh!" as if my shoulder had been hurt.

Danny immediately let go. I grabbed my shoulder and pretended it was hurt. I wasn't sure why I did that. I just knew that I didn't want to tap and acting like I was hurt was the only way I could think of not tapping.

"I'm sorry," Danny said. "Are you okay?"

"I think so," I said, rubbing my shoulder like it was hurt. "My arm just got caught in a weird position and I couldn't move it anymore."

"Oh, yeah. That move is called an omoplata," Danny said, nodding his head.

"What?"

"Yeah. That's a move. I learned it at my old school. It's called an omoplata. That means 'shoulder blade' in Portuguese, the language they speak in Brazil."

Then I heard Coach Adam from the side of the mat. He was standing next to Uncle Jake.

"Are you okay, Marc?" asked Coach Adam.

"I think so. My arm just got caught in a weird spot,"

I said, still trying to cover-up the fact that Danny had tapped me out with such a weird move.

"No," Coach Adam responded. "Your arm got caught in an omoplata. Nice work, Danny."

Great. Now EVEN COACH ADAM THOUGHT DANNY WAS SO COOL!

"Do you want me to show it to you? It really isn't that hard once you get the hang of it." Now Danny was trying to be my instructor too!

"No thanks. My shoulder   hurts," I said as I rubbed my shoulder some more.

"I'm really sorry about that, Marc. I was expecting you to tap out and then, all of a sudden, you just yelled out in pain," Danny said, looking very concerned for me—almost like he was MY MOM! This was RIDICULOUS!

"It's fine," I told him. "I'll be just fine."

I slowly got up off the mat, being very careful with my shoulder, holding my arm close to my chest like I could barely keep it up.

"Let's go. We'll get some ice on that when we get home," Uncle Jake said.

"Okay, thanks, Uncle Jake," I replied.

I said goodbye to Coach Adam and the rest of the people in class and headed for the door, still nursing my arm very carefully.

As we walked down the stairs, out the door and over to where our car was parked, I started thinking about what was going on and I didn't feel very good about it at all. This was a lie. I was pretending to be hurt. I start-

-ed thinking about how bad that would make Danny feel. I started to think about the jiu-jitsu team and how much I was letting them down by not being at practices and not training with them because of my fake hurt arm.

Just as we got to the car, Uncle Jake stopped walking. I took a few more steps toward the car, but then turned around to see what he was doing. He was just standing there looking at me. Then, without warning, he threw the car keys at me pretty hard and yelled, "CATCH!"

Without thinking, I reflexively reached up above my head and caught the keys. Uncle Jake stood there looking at me as I stood there with my hand over my head, the keys in my grip.

Uncle Jake looked at me, then looked at my hand, then back at me, then back at my hand again. I didn't have any idea why he was looking at me so strangely.

Then it hit me: I had caught the keys in my hand with my bad shoulder. Just as I started to lower it, Uncle Jake said, "You aren't even hurt, are you, Marc?" in the most direct possible way. It actually scared me. And he was right. My arm was fine.

But there was another part of me that was hurt. And now I felt completely awful.

What kind of a kid pretends to get hurt to avoid tapping out? How could I have done that?

"I'm sorry, Uncle Jake," I told him.

"Sorry?" Uncle Jake asked with a disappointed look on his face. "Just get in the car."

"Yes, Uncle Jake," I said.

I felt miserable. And it was all because of Danny Rhinehart.

CHAPTER 11

We got in the car and Uncle Jake started it up. He didn't say anything. He just started driving. And since he wasn't saying anything, I just kind of sat there thinking. Boy, did I feel stupid. I had faked that my shoulder was hurt—but I really didn't know why. It wasn't just because I didn't want to tap out. I had tapped out millions of times in jiu-jitsu and it was fine. That was actually a great way to learn for the next time.

So what was bothering me so much about tapping out this time? I wondered to myself.

I guess Uncle Jake was wondering the same thing.

"Why?" he finally asked as we drove down the road. But the weird thing with Uncle Jake was that most of the time when he asked a question, he already knew the answer. I didn't know what the answer was.

"I don't know, Uncle Jake," I told him.

"Yes, you do," he replied. "You just don't see it yet—or want to admit it."

"Admit what, Uncle Jake?" I asked him. I really had no idea what my problem was.

"Admit that you are jealous of Danny Rhinehart."

"Me?! Jealous of Danny? No way! I don't even like Danny Rhinehart! Why would I be jealous of him?"

"Because of your ego. Do you know what an ego is?"

"I have no idea, Uncle Jake."

Uncle Jake was quiet for a minute. Then he said, "Your ego is you. It is your thoughts and feelings and how you see yourself and how you see others. It is how you think you fit into the world. And it is what you think of yourself."

"I don't think I understand," I said.

Wait, you're my ego.
But you're me... ?

"Well, let me put it to you like this. If someone has a big ego, that means they think they are the greatest thing in the world. They think they are better than other people. They think they deserve to be at the top. If someone's ego is too small, then they lack confidence. They don't think they can do well—they don't think they can win."

"A person's ego should be balanced in the middle somewhere. They should have confidence, but not be over-confident. They should believe they can win, but at the same time know they are going to have to work hard to get there. So ego isn't good or bad, it is just something you have to learn to control."

"Okay, Uncle Jake. I think I get what you are talking about. A person shouldn't think they are the best thing in the world, but they shouldn't think they are the worst either. Is that right?" I asked.

"Yeah, that's it. And if ego goes too far in one direction or the other, it is a problem. If you think you are the greatest, you don't work as hard or train as hard because you believe you are the best—so you end up losing. If you think you are the worst, you won't have any confidence and you will get shaken up when things go wrong—so you end up losing. So, like I said, you have to keep your ego balanced in the middle. Confident, but not cocky."

It's all about balance.

"Okay. I get it, Uncle Jake. But what does this have to do with Danny Rhinehart and me?"

Uncle Jake took a deep breath. "The problem you have with Danny is that he is good at everything. He is smart. He is fast. He is strong. He is even good at jiu-jitsu.

And on top of all that, he is actually a pretty nice kid. His being so good at everything bothers your ego. Your ego wants YOU to be the best. But your ego sees that Danny can beat you in a lot of things. And that hurts your ego. That bothers your ego. It bothers you too. So you don't like Danny, but you don't even know why. But the answer is obvious to me. You are jealous of him. And that is caused by your ego."

I'm not such a bad guy...

I didn't even know what to say. I just sat there. We pulled into the driveway at my house. I didn't open the door because I knew the conversation wasn't over yet. I still needed to figure this out. Uncle Jake knew that too.

Finally, he asked, "What is it you don't like about Danny?"

I still didn't know what to say.

"Is he mean? Does he bully? Does he pick on kids? Is

he rude or obnoxious?"

As usual, I could tell Uncle Jake already knew the answer to these questions.

"No," I answered, "he's not any of those things."

"What is it then?" Uncle Jake asked.

Once again, I could tell Uncle Jake knew the answer to this question. So I figured I might as well admit it.

"Well. I guess I am jealous of him," I confessed. Then I just got really emotional—I couldn't help it. "He's just so good at everything!" I admitted, as tears started to come out of my eyes. I was totally embarrassed, but I couldn't help it.

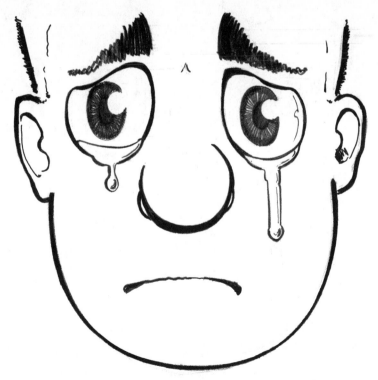

"He's good at running and math and pull-ups and even jiu-jitsu. And my friends that used to look up to me—Nathan and Kenny—now they look up to him even more. And it just doesn't feel very good to work so hard and come up short in EVERYTHING."

Uncle Jake sat quietly, then he kind of chuckled—he laughed!

"What are you laughing at, Uncle Jake?!?" I asked him.

He laughed a little bit more, then shook his head and said, "Ego."

"What? Why is that funny?" I asked.

"It's funny because I've seen the same thing so many times—ego causing all kinds of problems. It caused me more problems than you can imagine. And it is going to keep causing you problems until you get it under control. Guess what, you aren't going to be the best at everything all the time. You aren't going to beat every-one and be smarter than everyone. That's not the way things work. And if you let it bother you this much, you will always feel like this—angry at yourself—angry at other people. Angry at the world. But if you can control your ego—put your ego in check when it needs to be put in check and allow it to be strong when it needs to be—you won't be angry, you'll be happy. You'll do better. And you'll be a better person."

It all started to make sense now. But I wasn't sure where to go with it. I thought about it a bit. Then I asked Uncle Jake, "How do I learn to get control of my ego?"

Uncle Jake smiled and said, "You become friends with Danny Rhinehart."

That wasn't the answer I wanted to hear.

I didn't like that idea at all. But I knew that Uncle Jake was right.

CHAPTER 12

I stayed up late thinking about everything Uncle Jake had told me. I knew he was right; it all made sense. But then in the morning when we were working out, he told me something that seemed crazy.

As I was doing pull-ups, I heard Uncle Jake come closer to me.

"So that arm wasn't really even hurt at all, was it?"

"Not really, Uncle Jake."

"You need to apologize to Danny and Coach Adam," he said gravely.

"What?" I asked, knowing that this would make me look horrible.

"I said you need to apologize to Danny and Coach Adam. For faking the arm injury. For causing drama. For making Danny feel bad about hurting you and making Coach Adam worry. You need to apologize."

"But, I..." I stuttered as I started to try and figure out how I was going to get out of this one.

"But what?" Uncle Jake interjected. "You lied. There is no excuse for lying. When you don't tell the truth, it will always come back to haunt you. And lying is disrespectful to others and will destroy any level of trust you can have with a person. Being trustworthy is one of the most important characteristics a person can have. On the battlefield you have to trust the people you work with. And if you lie, it can get people killed. Do you understand that, Marc?"

"Yes, Uncle Jake. I do." I felt HORRIBLE. Of course, my parents had told me that lying was bad, but I had never really realized how truly awful it was to lie.

What was I thinking...

"Good. Now, you need to apologize. To them both. Tonight. At practice."

That was it. When Uncle Jake got that tone of voice, there was no getting around it. "Yes, Uncle Jake, I will," even though I hated the thought of it.

We kept working out and didn't say anything else. As I worked out, I thought about everything that had happened. And more stuff started to make sense. First of all—I should not have told a lie. It made me feel AWFUL. I also started to realize that it was my ego again that was making me not want to apologize. My ego didn't want to admit that I had lied. My ego didn't want me to look stupid and untrustworthy. So I didn't want to say anything.

You're letting your ego get the best of you.

When we finished working out, Uncle Jake looked at me with a serious expression. "You are going to become friends with Danny, right?"

"Yeah, I am, Uncle Jake," I responded, knowing that was what I had said I would do.

"Do you know what makes people friends?" he asked.

"They hang around with each other?" I responded, thinking that's what made me friends with Nathan and Kenny.

"No," Uncle Jake replied. "That's not it. Friends trust each other. To build trust you tell the truth. Even if it hurts your ego. That's what you have to do tonight."

"Okay," I told him.

That night when we got to jiu-jitsu, I walked into the academy. Coach Adam had a surprised look on his face.

"I didn't expect to see you for a few days," he said. "I figured your arm was hurt pretty bad."

I looked to the ground, then over at Uncle Jake. Uncle Jake just nodded at me—his way of saying it was time for me to tell the truth.

I took a deep breath. "I didn't get hurt, Coach Adam."

"What?" Coach Adam replied, with a puzzled look on his face.

"I'm not hurt," I said again, "and I didn't get hurt yesterday."

"Well, then what were the yell and the icepack and the holding all about?" Coach Adam asked in a pretty frustrated tone.

"I faked it, Coach Adam."

"You faked it?!" Coach Adam exclaimed.

"Yes, I did Coach Adam. I'm sorry," I told him.

"Let me guess. You didn't want Danny to tap you out with that move?"

"Yes. He has tapped me out before. But—I didn't even know what he was doing was a real move. And I have been training. And I've tapped him a few times too. And...well...."

"Ego," Coach Adam said, "that's your ego." Uncle Jake nodded his head.

"Yes, it is, Coach Adam. Uncle Jake explained what ego is to me. And this was definitely my ego getting the best of me."

"That's a shame. I hope you can put your ego in check. Because if you and Danny train together and actually help each other, you will both get a lot better—very quickly. You need to be pushing each other. And you need to keep your ego off the mat!"

"I will, Coach Adam," I told him, "I will."

"And you need to apologize to Danny. He felt really bad and believed that he had hurt you."

"I will, Coach," I said.

"Yes, you will," Coach replied, then he looked over on the mat where Danny was warming up, and yelled, "Danny! Come over here!"

Danny jogged off the mat and came over to where we were all standing.

"Marc has something to tell you, Danny," Coach said.

"I'm really sorry about your arm, Marc. I didn't mean—"

"It's okay, Danny," I cut him off. He didn't need to apologize to me. I needed to apologize to him. "Danny, I actually need to apologize to you." He looked at me, very confused. "You see, you didn't hurt my shoulder. At all."

"I didn't?" Danny asked.

"No. You didn't. I wasn't hurt. I just pretended to be hurt so I didn't have to tap. I didn't think that what you were doing was a real move, and I was embarrassed and didn't want to tap out. So I just yelled and pretended to be hurt. That was the wrong thing to do—and I'm sorry."

Danny kind of smiled. Only this time, it seemed like he was truly being nice. "It's okay. There are times I don't like to tap either. I'm just glad you are okay, because you're really good at jiu-jitsu and I want to keep training with you."

I was surprised. Danny was still being nice to me, even though I had lied to him and made him feel bad thinking he had hurt me.

Now that I had started to understand my ego and get it under control, I realized how jealous I had really been of him. And I realized that he hadn't been the problem. I had been.

"Thanks, Danny. I am really sorry. And I want to keep training with you. And I don't care if you tap me out or not—it will just help me learn." Uncle Jake smiled at me.

"That's exactly what I think," Danny said.

"Alright then, boys, enough talking," Coach Adam said. "Get out there and train."

Danny and I walked out to that mat, shook hands, and started training.

And even if I didn't beat Danny, I knew that I was at least beating my ego.

CHAPTER 13

When I woke up this morning, I was feeling pretty good. I had some good training with Danny yesterday, and I felt better now that I had told the truth to him and Coach Adam. And I have to admit that now that I knew it was my ego that had made me not like Danny, I could see he actually might be a pretty nice kid.

But all that good feeling was tested when I did my workout with Uncle Jake this morning. First we did a bunch of pull-ups, push-ups, sit-ups, burpees, and jumping jacks. Jumping jacks always seem easy when I start them—but try doing a hundred of them in a row!!!

When we finished the workout in the garage, I thought I was going to take a little break, have some breakfast, and relax before Nathan and Kenny came over to go get our work done for the day. Because we had four houses worth of yard work to take care of, it was going to be a busy day.

So, when I completed the final set of exercises, I said, "Thanks! That was a great workout!"

"It's not over yet," he replied. "We are going to do some interval training."

"Interval training? I haven't heard of that. What is it?"

"It will be easier to show you than to tell you," Uncle Jake said. "It will make you faster. But it may hurt a little bit while it is happening."

At this point, I got a little nervous. When Uncle Jake said something was going to hurt "a little bit", that meant it was going to hurt A TON for a normal person— like me!

"Okay, Uncle Jake," I said.

I must have not sounded very motivated, because Uncle Jake said, "Well, with an attitude like that, it might hurt a lot. Come on. Get in the game. This interval training will make you faster. Let's go."

At this point, Uncle Jake started to jog, and I followed him. But he wasn't running very fast; in fact, he was jogging at a pretty slow pace. As he jogged, he told me, "Interval training means that we are going to go easy for a bit, then hard—really hard—for a little bit, then easy for a while, then hard again, then easy again, and we are going to keep doing that for a while. Got it?"

"Okay," I told him.

"Good, first hard sprint is going to be from the mailbox there up to that next corner right ahead, got it?" he said, pointing at the mailbox and the corner up ahead.

"Okay," I said. We jogged a little bit farther until we got to the mailbox and BOOM! Uncle Jake took off at a full sprint!

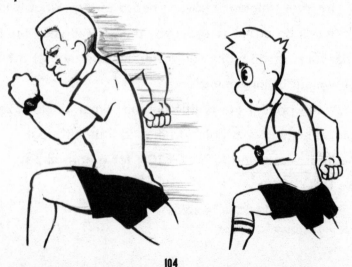

I followed him as close as I could, sprinting as fast as I could go. The sprint didn't take very long, and when I got to the corner, I slowed back down and caught up to Uncle Jake.

"Next one is from that brick driveway to that big tree, okay?" Uncle Jake said.

"Got it," I told him.

When we got to the brick driveway, we sprinted again, and I was going as fast as I possibly could all the way to the big tree. These sprints were tough, but they weren't very long, so I realized I could run with every-thing I had—there wasn't any reason to save any energy.

I'm just going to crank my output level to 'high'!

And we kept doing that. Jogging. Sprinting. Jogging. Sprinting. Jogging. Sprinting...over and over again. I was getting tired, but it was a different kind of tired than I would get when running the mile. This workout made me feel good.

Eventually, we turned and were headed back toward the house. During the middle of the run, some of the sprints were a little longer, but as we got closer to the house, Uncle Jake made the sprints shorter and shorter so I could still sprint FAST the whole time.

Finally, we got back to the house. My legs were a little sore, but the run had made me feel really good—and fast.

"How'd you like that, Marc?" Uncle Jake asked me.

"Awesome. It was kind of fun to be able to sprint so fast."

"Good. It is a great workout—and it will make you faster on your mile time too. We'll do this type of workout every few days to get your speed up, okay?"

"Sounds good, Uncle Jake," I said as he raised his hand and I gave him a high five.

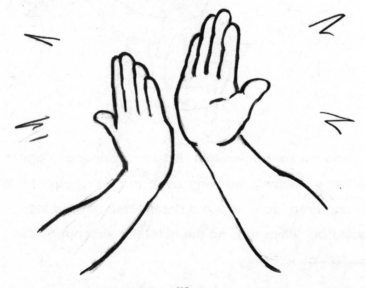

Finally, I went and got ready for the workday. Right at eight o'clock, Kenny and Nathan arrived. They were ready to work! We loaded up the wagon and got busy.

And it was a good thing we did, because we had tons of work, especially at the Vandenberg's house. They were a new customer, and we hadn't worked on their yard at all. So it was a MESS! We had to pull out all kinds of weeds, and we actually had to mow the lawn, rake it, and then mow it again! It took a long time.

By the time we were done with the Vandenberg's house, it was already late. We didn't even take any breaks or stop for lunch—we just kept working.

"We are going to have to hurry if we are going to get done in time for jiu-jitsu," Kenny said. He was right; we were running late.

"Yes, we are—let's have a weed race!" Nathan said. "Whoever pulls the most, wins!"

At the next house, we all got buckets and started pulling weeds as fast as we could. Every time we would fill our buckets, we would run over and put them in a separate pile. After about fifteen minutes, there were no more weeds to pick up!

"You won it, Nathan," I said, looking at his pile of weeds, which was slightly bigger than mine and Kenny's.

"YES! I am the weed pulling king!" Nathan shouted as he picked up some weeds and put them on his head like a crown.

We laughed and then Kenny said, "Come on! We have to finish up."

So we all got back to work, mowed the lawn, raked and swept up. We were done but without much time to spare. We loaded up the wagon and headed back to my house.

"Looks like we are going to make it," Kenny said.

"But it will be close," Nathan added.

"Maybe we should get someone else to help?" Kenny suggested.

"How about Danny?" Nathan asked quietly, and the way he asked, it sounded like maybe he thought I wouldn't like that idea. Maybe he thought I was jealous of Danny. But he didn't know I had my ego under control now.

"Good idea!" I said cheerfully. "I can ask him tonight!"

"Cool," said Nathan.

"Awesome," said Kenny.

I was excited. This was a good way to become better friends with Danny, a good way to get some extra help for Marc's Meticulous Mowing, and a good way to make sure my ego was under control.

CHAPTER 14

I am supposed to be making friends with Danny. And I am really trying. I realize that the biggest problem in making friends with him is me and my ego. So I am doing my best to be nice and really become friends with him.

One way to do that was an idea from Uncle Jake. He told me to show Danny my best jiu-jitsu moves! At first I didn't like that idea one bit! "If I show him my moves, I'll never be able to tap him out!"

"Wrong, Marc. If you show him your moves, he will learn to defend them. Once he knows how to defend them, they won't work. If they won't work, you will have to use another move to get him—and that will make you better. Also, if you show him your moves, he will most likely show you his moves. Then you can defend against his moves, and that will make him better too. And the more moves you both learn to use and defend—the better you will both get!"

And we'll become better friends!

And I'll become better at tapping you out!

So, even though I didn't really want to, when I got to jiu-jitsu, I went over to Danny and asked, "Hey, Danny, remember when I made you tap with a choke a couple weeks ago?"

"Yeah," he replied, "that was a good move. I wish you knew what you did so we could learn it. But you said you didn't really know and just got lucky and squeezed. But it was a tight choke!"

"Well, I actually do know what I did," I told him.

"Really?" he responded, with a surprised look on his face.

"Yeah, really," I said. "It was the only time I had made you tap and I figured if I told you how, I wouldn't be able to get you with it again—and you might use it to get me!"

I thought Danny might be mad, but he just laughed and said, "You might be right about that! But if you teach your training partners the moves you know, it makes you better!"

"I know, I know. But I wasn't thinking about that! Anyway, the move I got you in was called the 'loop choke'."

"The loop choke?" Danny asked.

"Yes. The loop choke. It's kind of a tricky move. Let me show you how to do it." At that point, I explained the loop choke to Danny. I showed him where to put his hands and how to place his grip. I even showed him how to trick the person into thinking they are passing your guard when you are really just about to choke them! Danny loved it!

Then Danny said, "Let me show you the omoplata!"

This was the move that Danny had done to me before I faked getting hurt so I wouldn't have to tap.

This move was pretty crazy! It was a way of trapping the arm by just using your legs and it was very sneaky. It was a much harder move than the loop choke and it took me a bunch of tries before I finally made it work. But it was a really cool move!

"That's awesome," I told Danny.

Then I spent some time telling Danny how he could avoid getting caught in the loop choke by simply ducking his head under my hand before he passed my guard. And Danny showed me some ways to defend against and even escape from the omoplata. It was so cool!

Once we taught each other the loop choke and the omaplata, we started showing each other some different moves and going over little details that made the moves work. It was really helpful. I was surprised at how much Danny taught me and how much I taught him.

But things didn't go the way I thought they would. After we finished showing each other moves, I figured it was a good time to ask Danny if he wanted to help out with Marc's Meticulous Mowing.

"Nathan, Kenny, and I work every day mowing lawns and pulling weeds, and we have a lot of work to do and we could use an extra hand. Do you think you might want to come over to my house tomorrow and help us? We start at eight o'clock in the morning. You have to wear some clothes that you don't mind getting dirty and bring a water bottle with you and maybe a snack, too, in case you get hungry."

Danny had a weird look on his face.

He looked like he really wanted to do it, but then he looked disappointed and said, "Sorry, Marc. Thanks for asking, but I am going to be doing some stuff with my older brother tomorrow."

I was thinking maybe it sounded like too much work— then I realized I forgot to tell him the best part! "One more thing I forgot to tell you, Danny. You get paid! All the different families pay me to take care of their lawns—and we split up that money!"

I thought this would convince Danny.

"Woah!" Danny said, "that's awesome." He looked excited for a second, then he looked disappointed again, and said, "But I am going to be hanging around with my older brother tomorrow."

Okay, I figured. Danny had some stuff to do tomorrow. I guess that was understandable. But not a big problem. "No problem. How about the next day?" I asked him.

"Well, I'm going to be busy with my brother on that day as well," he answered.

"What about the day after that?" I asked.

"I'll probably being doing something with my brother on that day as well. Sorry, Marc."

At this point I kind of gave up. It didn't make any sense to me. I was being super nice to Danny. We had taught each other our best jiu-jitsu moves. But he still didn't want to come over and help us work. Maybe Danny was just lazy. Maybe he was only pretending to like me so that he could get my jiu-jitsu moves!

There's something awfully strange about this kid.

I wasn't sure what the problem was, but it seemed like Danny must have some reason he didn't want to come and help us work. Maybe Danny wasn't as 'nice' as he was acting. And I didn't like that one bit.

CHAPTER 15

"How is it going with Danny?" Uncle Jake asked as he did some push-ups during our morning workout.

"I don't know," I replied.

"You don't know? Why not? I hope you're not letting your ego get in the way," he said as I did my set of squat-jumps.

"I'm not letting my ego get in the way, Uncle Jake," I said, breathing hard from my set, "but I'm not sure Danny is as nice as he seems."

"What makes you think that, Marc?" Uncle Jake asked.

I stopped working out for a second so I could explain the situation to Uncle Jake. "Well, I asked him yesterday if he wanted to come over to-day and help Kenny and Nathan and me with the lawns. He said no. Then I asked him about the next day. He said no. Then I asked him about the day after that, and he still said no! I would say maybe he is lazy and doesn't want to work, but, he is at jiu-jitsu every day working hard, so I don't think that is it. I think maybe he just doesn't like me or Kenny or Nathan."

"Do your push-ups," Uncle Jake said. I guess I had been talking a little too long.

"This is the same thing you went through with Nathan. There's no telling what is going on in Danny's life. Don't be so quick to judge," Uncle Jake said.

I kept doing my push-ups, but I had to answer this. "I've already gathered some intelligence about Danny because I knew you might say this!" I said to Uncle Jake with a smile on my face.

Uncle Jake smiled back. "Okay, what did you find out."

"Well his parents have a really nice car. In fact, at

least two really nice cars—when his mom drops him off she drives one nice car, when his dad drops him off, he drives another one. Both of the cars look brand new! He also has really nice sneakers. And he has already had two new pairs, just this summer! On top of that, he has a bunch of nice jiu-jitsu gis and even a special jiu-jitsu backpack that he brings to the gym! A special back-pack—just for jiu-jitsu!"

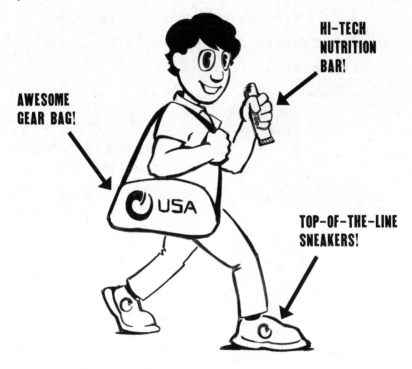

AWESOME GEAR BAG!

HI-TECH NUTRITION BAR!

TOP-OF-THE-LINE SNEAKERS!

"And in that backpack he has nice little snacks. Sand-wiches, other snacks, and even one of those really nice water bottles that keeps drinks cold. He has EVERYTHING!" I told Uncle Jake as I finished my set of push-ups.

Uncle Jake listened as he was doing his set of jump squats. He was breathing hard, but I could see a little smile on his face. He was impressed that I had gathered such good intelligence about Danny, just like Uncle Jake had me do last year when I gathered intelligence about Nathan. But with Nathan, what I learned was completely different. Nathan was living a very rough life. He didn't have money for food or clothes, and he had to return cans and bottles to buy things to eat. His dad wasn't around and his mom had to work all the time so she wasn't home much.

I may not be rich but I've got great friends, a great job and a great future!

Danny's life was completely different. Like I had told Uncle Jake, he seemed to have EVERYTHING he could want! Cars and food and clothes—everything! And there was one more thing I hadn't told Uncle Jake yet. "One more thing, Uncle Jake," I said.

"What's that?" he replied.

"Guess what kind of bike Danny Rhinehart has?"

Uncle Jake looked at me like he knew the answer. He didn't say anything, but I could tell he knew.

"That's right! He has a Bentlee bike! The same exact one I wanted last year. The most expensive bike in the shop. So I don't think Danny is exactly living a rough life!" I told Uncle Jake with a smile on my face.

Uncle Jake just nodded.

Finally! It started to seem like maybe I was right about Danny and maybe he wasn't as nice as Uncle Jake seemed to think he was.

Uncle Jake remained silent the rest of the workout as we finished our sets of push-ups and squats. Once we were done, Uncle Jake looked at me and said, "Alright, let's go do your run."

We walked out of the garage and to the driveway.

"Let's give it a good push today," Uncle Jake said, "and while you run, I want you to think about what you learned from Nathan last year. Okay?"

"Okay," I said.

"Standby...BUST 'EM!"

I took off running at a good pace. Uncle Jake stayed just ahead of me, but I struggled and stayed pretty close. I could tell that I was running a bit faster than normal. The sprints from the interval training were really helping out, and I could feel it.

At the turn around point, Uncle Jake ran past me back toward the house, "Keep it up!" he said with a stern look on his face.

I tried. But as I got to the bottom of the hill and headed back toward the finish line at my driveway, I slowed down just a little tiny bit. Uncle Jake seemed just too far ahead to keep up with.

When I finally crossed the finish line, Uncle Jake said, "Six-fourteen."

Six minutes and fourteen seconds. That was my fastest time yet.

YES!!!

"Yes!" I shouted, "A new record!"

Uncle Jake just looked at me. "Not bad," he said.

"Thanks Unc..."

"But not good," Uncle Jake cut me off. "You can do better."

"How much better?" I asked, wondering if I would ever be good enough for Uncle Jake's standards.

"You can get a sub-six-minute mile," he replied flatly.

"Sub-six?" I asked him, wondering exactly what that meant.

"Less than six minutes. You can do a mile in less that six minutes. That is the goal. Okay?"

"Of course, Uncle Jake. That sounds pretty cool," I told him, and it did sound pretty cool.

"Well, it won't feel cool, Marc," Uncle Jake said. "You have already done the easy part—getting to where you are pretty fast. You have shaved a bunch of time off your mile run. But to shave off more now is going to be hard. You are going to have to earn every second you get off that time. It is going to take hard work. *Really hard work.* Okay?"

"Yes, Uncle Jake. I'll work hard."

"Good," Uncle Jake replied, and then he stood quiet for a minute, but I could tell he had something else to say.

"Now. What did you learn from Nathan James last year?"

This seemed like such an easy question. "I learned that some people have a rougher life than me. Nathan didn't have much money for food or clothes. He had to return cans and bottles to buy his lunch and dinner. His life was tough and I needed to understand how hard it was to live without much money."

Uncle Jake shook his head. He wasn't happy with my answer.

"Wrong," he said. "That's only part of the lesson. The

more important lesson is that you don't know what is going on with people in their lives and you shouldn't judge them. Sure, Nathan and his family don't have much money, but that isn't the only hardship people can face. There are all kinds of things people have to go through. Right now, you are judging Danny, thinking he is lazy or doesn't like you, but you don't actually know what is going on in his life."

"But I do," I told Uncle Jake quickly, proud of the information I had gathered about Danny, "I already told you, he has plenty of money! Shoes and bikes and cars and backpacks—he has everything!"

TOP SECRET
Danny
Rhinehart
Files

"I just told you," Uncle Jake said with a serious look on his face, "life isn't all about money. Money isn't the only problem people have and money doesn't solve every hardship. There is more to life than just money. You need to get to know Danny a little better before you judge him. Do you understand me?"

"Okay, Uncle Jake," I said. I wasn't quite sure what Uncle Jake meant, but he seemed a little aggravated with me, so I figured I should just listen to what he was saying so I could try to figure it out. But even as I thought about it, I couldn't understand why Danny wouldn't want to come over and help us. It didn't make sense.

CHAPTER 16

Today Nathan, Kenny and I had a TON of work to do. When we completed our first house, we had to go immediately to the next one, and then the next one and the next. By lunch time, we had worked four houses and still had four more to do.

I know Uncle Jake wanted me to be friends with Danny and all that, but today I just had had enough and couldn't help from saying something about it to Nathan and Kenny.

"I can't believe Danny won't help us! I wonder what he does all day?!?"

Nathan and Kenny laughed. Then Kenny got a serious look on his face and said, "I wonder what he does do?"

"He always says he's 'doing something with his older brother,'" I told them.

Just who is this brother of his...

"Everyday?" Nathan asked.

"That's what he tells me," I replied.

"Who would want to hang around your older brother all day every day?" Kenny asked.

"Yeah! No kidding," Nathan added, and then continued, saying, "and what about the money? We are making a lot of money! Doesn't he want the money?"

"Yeah! Who doesn't need money?" Kenny said.

Y'know, you took the words, right out of my mouth!

Nathan and Kenny stood there shaking their heads. I know I was supposed to be keeping my ego under control, but honestly, it felt kind of good to hear Kenny and Nathan realizing that maybe Danny wasn't so perfect after all! I felt a little bad, because I knew Uncle Jake wouldn't want me to be saying anything bad about Danny. But, at the same time, everything I was saying was true! Why should I feel bad about saying something that is actually true? So I explained some more things about Danny, "I think Danny doesn't need money."

"What?" Nathan said with a surprised look on his face, "Who doesn't need money?"

"Danny," I replied. "Have you seen his parents' cars? The kind of shoes he wears? The Bentlee bike he rides? Even his backpack is a super-nice, brand new jiu-jitsu backpack! I don't think he needs any money at all! His parents are rich, and it seems like they give him whatever he wants!"

SUPER RICH KID ALERT!

"Yeah," Nathan said shaking his head, "now that you mention it, he does seem to have pretty much everything."

"Spoiled!" Kenny shouted.

I didn't answer that or agree with it out loud. I knew that was going a little too far. But, inside, I felt the same way and my ego was sure happy to hear these guys finally understanding that Danny was not the kind of person to look up to.

"Well," I finally said, "The bottom line is he isn't here, and he isn't going to be here, and all this talking won't get these lawns taken care of, so we better get to work!"

Nathan and Kenny agreed and we packed up the wagon and headed to the next house and then the next and finally, the last one.

By the time we were done, we pretty much went straight to jiu-jitsu.

Once we were there, I figured I had better make another attempt at getting to know Danny better, so I invited him to work with us again.

"We were working all day today, Danny, and we could really use some help. Are you sure you can't help us tomorrow?"

Just as I expected, Danny said the same old thing, "Sorry, Marc. But I'm going to be doing some things with my brother tomorrow pretty much the whole day."

"Okay," I said. Then I thought to myself, *Maybe Danny just doesn't want to work. After all, he has plenty of money.* So I changed tactics.

"What about after jiu-jitsu tomorrow? Do you want to come over and just hang out?"

I could have guessed it! Danny said the same thing, "Well, I'll be hanging around with my brother tomorrow after jiu-jitsu."

"What about the next night? Same thing? Hanging around with your brother?" I asked, showing that I was not really believing him.

We can do this the easy way, or the hard way, Danny...

"Well, yeah, actually. That is what I am doing."

"Is that all you ever do, Danny? Hang around your brother? Doesn't it get boring? Don't you want to hang out with us kids?"

Danny sat there for a minute, looking a little bit sad. I didn't get it at all! Why would he be sad? He was the one that didn't want to do anything with the rest of us.

Then he finally said, "Why don't you come over to my house tomorrow after jiu-jitsu. I have to check with my parents, but it should be okay. That way you can meet my brother."

That kind of surprised me. I didn't understand why he didn't want to come to my house, but didn't mind me going over to his house. And, I knew Uncle Jake wanted me to learn more about Danny, so I figured I better just go.

"Okay. I'll have to check with my mom, but she won't mind."

"Great. I'll get your phone number and call you when

I get home to make sure my mom says it's okay."

That was that. After we talked, we trained some more and we trained pretty hard. I didn't tap him out, but he didn't tap me out either. And, of course, as usual, he was super nice to me the whole time. When we finished, I gave him the phone number to my house.

"Well, he's not coming over," I told Uncle Jake when I got in the car to head home.

"Did you–" Uncle Jake started to ask me a question, but I cut him off–something I don't do very often!

"But I'm going over to his house!"

Uncle Jake smiled. "Nice work. When?"

"Should be tomorrow after jiu-jitsu. He is going to call tonight to make sure his mom says it is okay."

"Perfect," Uncle Jake said.

We got home, made dinner, and were sitting at the table eating when the phone rang.

"I got it!" I said, knowing it was for me as I got up from the table and picked up the phone.

Just as I thought, it was Danny. He said his mom had said it was okay if I came over the next night after jiu-jitsu. I sat back down at the table.

"Well?" Uncle Jake asked me.

"I'm going," I told him.

"Perfect," he said, "now you can learn something about what makes Danny tick."

"Yes, Uncle Jake," I replied. And I was starting to really wonder the answer to that exact question. I guess I'll find out tomorrow.

CHAPTER 17

What happened today was very unexpected, but I sure learned a lot. We had a pretty light day of work, but had fun doing it. Kenny and Nathan are really fun to have around. When we finished, Kenny and Nathan headed home, and I cleaned up, got ready for jiu-jitsu and brought a change of clothes so I could go over to Danny's house afterward.

Jiu-jitsu was fun too. We did "monkey in the middle" with takedowns, where the person that got taken down leaves the mat and a new person comes in to challenge the person that won. I did pretty well—but it is very tiring and, eventually, everyone gets taken down.

After practice, we cleaned the mats and I changed clothes. Danny was waiting for me and we walked outside to his car. His car was really nice.

"This is my mom," he said, "Mom, this is Marc."

"Nice to meet you Mrs. Rhinehart," I told her as I got in the car.

"Nice to meet you too, Marc," she responded with a nice smile.

They didn't live too far from the gym, and as we drove, Danny and I were laughing about one of the takedowns I had tried to do, but accidentally fell and was immediately out.

As we pulled into Danny's driveway, it was just as I expected. The house was HUGE and completely perfect. It looked like a mansion. And the yard was very well taken care of—they had no need for Marc's Meticulous Mowing.

As soon as we went inside, I heard someone yelling, "DANNY! DANNY!"

It was Danny's brother, and he came running down the stairs toward us. As soon as I saw him, I could tell there was something different about him.

"Hi, Danny!" Danny's brother shouted. "Who is that?" he asked, pointing at me. His voice was a little hard to understand as he kind of blurred the words together, sounding almost like he had some food in his mouth while he was talking.

"That's a friend of mine," Danny answered.

"Hello friend."

"His name is Marc. Marc, this is my brother Anthony."

"Hi, Anthony," I said.

"Hi, Marc," he said back.

"Do you want to see my train collection?" Anthony asked.

"Sure," I said.

"GREAT!" Anthony replied as he ran up the stairs.

I looked at Danny, and Danny looked at me.

"He has a developmental disability," Danny said in a serious voice.

"Oh, okay," I replied, unsure of how to respond.

"It means he is developing slower than most kids. He can't do some of the stuff we can do and probably never will be able to. It also means he doesn't get to hang around other kids as much as we do. So, that's why I spend a lot of time with him."

I love you, brother!

I love you, too, brother!

Wow. Here I was this whole time, thinking that Danny just didn't want to hang around us other kids, and the whole time he was just taking care of his brother.

"DANNY! FRIEND! Come on up!" Anthony shouted, "I got the trains out!"

"Okay!" Danny yelled back. Then he looked at me and smiled. I smiled back.

"Let's go!" I said.

We went up the stairs and into a big giant playroom. I call it a play room because it wasn't a bedroom—there was no bed—it wasn't a living room—there were no couches—it was just a big giant room filled with toys.

And a lot of those toys were trains, the simple wooden trains with that come with a bunch of pieces of wooden tracks that link together to form big tracks.

"TRAINS!" Anthony shouted when we entered the room.

We sat down on the floor and started building a giant track. Danny was so nice and patient with his brother, it was amazing to see.

And we had fun! We built a crazy long track with
all kinds of curves, tunnels, and bridges, and then we
pushed the trains around the track and set up different
tracks and different trains. It was fun.

But at the same time, I realized, this is what Danny
did all the time. And even though it was fun to do for
an hour every once in a while, it had to be hard to do it
every day like Danny did.

"Does he like to do this every day?" I asked Danny.

"He sure does," Danny said back.

"Do you get bored?"

"Yeah, I do. But if I didn't play with him, especially in
the summer time, he really wouldn't have anyone to be
around. And beside, it makes me realize that I am very
lucky to be able to do what I do. We both are."

"Yes, we are," I replied.

We kept playing with the trains until Mrs. Rhinehart came up and said it was time for her to give me a ride home.

"Okay, Marc, I've got to take you home. Danny is going to stay with Anthony," she said.

"No problem," I replied.

I stood up and walked toward the door.

"I'll see you tomorrow, Danny," I said, "and I'll see you again sometime Anthony."

"See ya," Danny said.

"Wait!" Anthony shouted, then he ran over and gave me a hug. "Thanks for playing with me!"

"No problem, Anthony. Your trains are SUPER COOL!" I said with a smile.

"I know!" he said.

And with that I smiled and headed out the door. I followed Mrs. Rhinehart down to her car and she drove me home.

When we got to my house, I opened the door and got out.

"Thanks Mrs. Rhinehart," I told her looking back through the door.

"Thank you," she said back. "Thank you for being understanding. Danny really likes you and appreciates you being his friend. And thanks for being so nice to Anthony."

"No problem at all, Mrs. Rhinehart. It was fun."

With that she smiled and I closed the door.

Once in the house, I told Uncle Jake about Danny's house and about Anthony and about his disability and about the trains. I said that Danny spends all his time with Anthony because otherwise, no one else would.

After I told Uncle Jake everything, he looked at me and asked, "What did you learn?"

"Well, I learned about Danny's situation and about his brother," I said.

"But what did you learn about you?" he asked.

I wasn't quite sure what Uncle Jake meant by this.

At this point I"m an expert at solving mysteries.

I must have looked puzzled, because after a quiet moment, Uncle Jake said, "You should have learned a few things. You should have learned that just because people appear to have everything doesn't mean that their life is easy. You should have learned—once again—not to judge people without knowing them. On top of that, you should see your Warrior Kid Code number five, where you say 'A Warrior Kid always tries to help others.' Danny is really living that every day as he tries to help his brother. And, you also should have learned, like Danny has learned, that you are lucky to be healthy and that you need to take advantage of that and be the best you can every day."

"Yes, Uncle Jake, I learned those things too. All of them." And I meant it. I am lucky to be healthy, lucky to be able to run and swim and do jiu-jitsu and have my business. I am very lucky. And I need to always remember that.

CHAPTER 18

Today was pretty awesome! I woke up and did a great workout with Uncle Jake. We did all upper-body exercises: pull-ups, push-ups, sit-ups, dips, and a bunch of others. But we didn't do any burpees or squats or any leg exercises. I wasn't quite sure why.

"No leg exercises today?" I asked Uncle Jake.

"Not today. You are resting your legs today because tomorrow you are going to need them. Tomorrow you are going to try to run the mile in under six minutes. I want you to be ready," Uncle Jake explained.

"Got it! I will be!"

It will be more than this watch that you'll be racing against...

After we had worked out, Kenny and Nathan came over so we could get to work. They both knew I had gone to Danny's house, and they wanted to see if I had figured out why Danny didn't want to work with us—or hang around with us after jiu-jitsu.

"So what is his deal?" Kenny asked.

"Yeah, did you figure out why he doesn't want to help us?" Nathan added as we walked to the Kurth's house a few blocks away, towing our wagon of tools and supplies. When Nathan asked, I stopped walking.

"I did figure it out, guys," I said in a serious voice. "It's a good reason. You see Danny's older brother, Anthony, the one that he hangs around with all the time, has something called a developmental disability. So even though he is older than Danny, his mind isn't as advanced. He can't quite do things for himself. And it is hard for him to make friends and do some of the things that other kids do. So Danny spends a lot of time with him in the summer playing with him and being a good brother and friend. Trust me, Danny would love to do everything with us—but he also loves his brother and wants to take care of him."

"Woah," said Nathan, "that has got to be hard."

"I'm sure it is," Kenny said.

"Yeah, and boy, do I feel mean. The whole time I was thinking that Danny was weird just because he didn't want to hang around with us."

"Me too," Kenny said.

"Yep. Me too," Nathan echoed.

"Well, at least now we know and we can be nicer. My Uncle Jake pointed out that this is why you shouldn't judge people: you never know what they are going through."

"True," said Nathan as he nodded his head, probably recognizing that I had also judged him last summer for his bad attitude and sloppy clothes.

We all stood quietly for a moment before I said, "Well, let's get to work! These lawns aren't going to mow themselves!" We smiled, started walking, and soon got to work.

When we were done that afternoon, we headed off to jiu-jitsu class.

Before class started, Coach Adam told us to line up like we normally do.

As soon as we were lined up, Coach Adam, who was facing us said, "I have an announcement to make. Marc, come on out." I walked out of the line and faced Coach Adam.

"Turn around," he said, as he put his hand on my shoulder and turned me toward the class.

"As you all know, I have been waiting to select a team captain. And I have made my decision. Marc, I select you as the Victory Team Captain!"

"YES!" I thought to myself, "I AM THE TEAM CAPTAIN!"

I couldn't hold back the smile as I looked at the rest of the class. They all looked happy for me. Nathan and Kenny had huge smiles on their faces.

Then I looked at Danny. He didn't look happy—he was smiling at me, but at the same time I could tell that something was bothering him. Of course, he wanted to be captain too, and he was definitely as good or better at jiu-jitsu than me. But I had been at the school much longer, so I think that is why Coach Adam picked me. I felt bad, but it didn't seem there was anything I could do. Then I got an idea.

I turned around and faced Coach Adam.

"Coach," I said, "Thanks so much for picking me. But I think I might need some help being captain. Do you think there could be two captains of the team?"

"Of course, there can be. That's called co-captains."

"Awesome. And I think Danny would be the best. He is really good at jiu-jitsu and his attitude is great."

"I agree. Okay. Turn around," Coach said, and I turned back to face the class again.

"I have one more announcement," Coach Adam told the class. "Our team captain has pointed out that being team captain is a lot of work and responsibility—and that he might need some help doing the job. Therefore, he has requested that I appoint a co-captain to help him out. Danny, come on up here."

I watched Danny's face light up with happiness. He was smiling from ear to ear!

"Danny, you are now co-captain of the team with Marc," Coach said as Danny and I shook hands and then faced the class.

"Thanks, Coach," Danny said, and then he looked at me and said, "and thank you, Marc."

"You deserve it," I told Danny.

Then Coach looked at us both and asked, "Well?"

"Well what?" I asked.

"Well, how about you get your class warmed up so they can learn some moves and train!"

"Got it!" I said.

I looked at Danny and he just nodded.

"Okay! Time to warm up!" I said to the class in a loud voice. "Let's start jogging in a circle!"

The class began to jog around in a circle, and then we went through all our normal warm-up drills.

When we had finished our whole warm-up, I looked at Coach Adam and said, "All warmed-up, Coach!"

"Thanks, Marc," Coach said. Then he walked out on the mat and told us all to gather in closer so he could teach us the first move of the day—a review of the tri-ple-threat: kimura, sit-up sweep, and guillotine. After teaching and reviewing the moves, he said, "Alright, quick water break."

When the rest of the class went off the mat to get some water, he told Danny and me to run some spar-ring. He showed us how to work the countdown clock

and we programmed four-minute rounds. When everyone else was back on the mat, Danny said, "Okay, everyone, we are going to do five four-minute rounds! Grab a
partner!"

Everyone grabbed a partner; once everyone was
paired up, Danny pressed START on the clock and everyone started to train.

I looked at Danny and without saying a word, we
smiled, shook hands, and started to grapple.

It was a great day.

CHAPTER 19

Today I fell short of my goal.

For two days, Uncle Jake had me preparing to break the six-minute mile. One day we didn't work out any legs, and the next day he let me rest completely, and I just did some stretching. So today I was supposed to make it happen. I was supposed to run a mile in under six minutes. And I almost did. Almost.

"Almost" doesn't count when you're up against me, kid!

I woke up at the normal time, and Uncle Jake and I did a quick warm-up. We did few easy jumping jacks and burpees just to get our muscles warm, and then we stretched out.

"You ready?" Uncle Jake asked me.

"Yes, I am," I told him confidently.

"Alright then," he said. "Let's go!"

We walked down to the driveway and lined up for the start.

"Okay," he said, "today is the day. Standby..."

BUST 'EM!!

I took off running, and was running at a good solid pace. My breathing was steady and my stride was long. I was going just about as fast as Uncle Jake.

I made good time to the corner and started up the hill to the turnaround point. It almost seemed easy! Once I got to the fence, I slapped it and turned around. As soon as I did, Uncle Jake picked up his pace a little bit and pulled ahead. But I wasn't worried. I was running fast and didn't need to beat Uncle Jake to beat a six-minute mile.

On the way down the hill, I lengthened my stride and backed off my pace a little bit, so I could save some for the final sprint.

I don't like to brag, but I"m great at taking it easy, when I have to.

As Uncle Jake pulled even further ahead of me, I still thought I was running fast enough.

BUT I WASN'T.

I sprinted the last fifty yards and came across the finish line. I looked at Uncle Jake.

"Six thirteen," he said in a cold voice. "You didn't push yourself."

"I ran hard," I told him.

"Not that hard," he said directly. "Look at you right now. Standing. Talking. If you had really run hard, you would be exhausted. You would be sprawled out on the ground, trying to catch your breath."

I stood there silently. I didn't know what to say. I had let Uncle Jake down. And I had let myself down too.

We stood there for a few minutes. I was just looking at the ground, because I didn't even want to look at Uncle Jake. I had failed. I felt horrible.

"I failed a run once too," Uncle Jake finally said, breaking the silence. I looked at him, surprised to hear him say that.

"You did?" I asked.

There's NO WAY a bonafide Navy SEAL like Uncle Jake has ever failed!

"Yep," he answered, "I sure did. It was going through BUD/S, the basic SEAL training. I was in second phase, almost halfway done with the training. We ran all the time in BUD/S. It was a mile to the chow hall where we ate and a mile back—so just running to breakfast, lunch, and dinner, we were running six miles a day. On top of that, we ran everywhere we went, and, of course, we ran all kinds of regular "conditioning runs", which were the big group runs we did as a class to get us in shape. But once a week, we would do a four-mile timed run. Four miles isn't even that long—and the times we had to get to pass the runs weren't even that fast.

"But we were usually worn out for the runs, and they were in soft sand wearing combat boots."

Have you ever run in soft sand?"

"No I haven't, Uncle Jake," I told him.

"Well, it's pretty tough, but it isn't that big a deal," Uncle Jake continued. "Up until that point, I had passed all my runs."

Ok, I don't think I'd pass anything, running in sand.

So, one morning, when we lined up for the run, I decided that day I would 'pace myself'. Do you know what that means?"

"Hold back? Not run your hardest?" I replied.

"Exactly," Uncle Jake said. "Hold back a little bit—take it easy. After all, I figured, I hadn't had any trouble with the runs up until this point, and I figured I could save my energy for some of the other things we had to do like long swims and the obstacle course. So we all lined up for the run, and the instructor gave us the 'Standby…BUST 'EM'. And off we all ran. And don't get me wrong, I ran hard. But I held back. And when I crossed the finish line, the instructor simply said, 'Fail. Hit the surf and get wet and sandy.' That was the punishment for failing—you had to go jump in the ocean and then roll around in the sand so you looked like a sugar cookie."

What a coincidence. I'd give anything to look like a Navy SEAL!

COOKIES

But that wasn't the bad part. The bad part came later that afternoon when I, along with the rest of the people who had failed, had to go sign a chit stating that we failed."

"What's a chit?" I asked.

"It's a form for your record that says you failed. And when I went through BUD/S, if you failed two runs, you could be kicked out. I was petrified. I could NOT fail another run. And I didn't. The next timed run—I RAN. I ran as hard as I could. I didn't hold anything back. And that is what I did from then on. When it was go time—I went as hard as I could. I would finish the runs and collapse on the ground. And I never failed a run again. That's what you need to do next time. Don't hold anything back. 'Always do your best.' Isn't that what your Warrior Kid code says?"

I felt really bad. Uncle Jake was right. I could have run much harder, but I didn't. I looked up at him, "Yes, Uncle Jake. That is exactly what it says. And that is exactly what I will do. I promise."

"Good," said Uncle Jake, "That's what a Warrior Kid needs to do. And I'm not saying you need to do that all day every day. You shouldn't do that, and, in fact, you can't do that. Your body won't allow it. You have seen that happen—you can over train and get too tired. Your performance will go down. But on game day—when it is time to give it your all, then GIVE IT YOUR ALL. Go as HARD AS YOU CAN. Don't hold anything back. Do you understand what that means?"

"Yes, I do, Uncle Jake, yes, I do."

And I did. I was already looking forward to the next run, where I would get the chance to do just that.

CHAPTER 20

After training jiu-jitsu this whole summer, everything finally paid off!

The tournament went great. Nathan, Kenny, Danny, and I all entered the competition along with a few other kids from our academy, including Nora and Zisa, our two best girls. There were a lot of kids there from other jiu-jitsu schools and some of them were REALLY GOOD. My mom and dad had to work, but my Uncle Jake came to watch me, and Danny's parents came to watch him, and they brought Anthony with them. Anthony remembered me!

"Hello, friend!" he said when he saw me.

"Hello, Anthony," I replied.

"Are you going to win?" he asked.

"I am going to try," I told him.

"Danny is going to win!" he said with a big smile on his face.

"I am sure he will do great," I said.

In jiu-jitsu, you compete against people that are about the same weight as you. Nathan, Kenny, Danny and I were all in different weight classes. Kenny was the heaviest, then Danny, then me, and finally Nathan, who was the lightest.

As the team captains, Coach Adam had Danny and me warm the kids up before the competition. We told everyone to do their best and be good sports whether they won or lost.

Nathan went first and had a really tough match, but he was able to win by scoring points for taking his opponent down and getting the mount position.

I won my first match using an armlock, and Danny also made his first opponent tap out, but he used a choke. Kenny also beat his first opponent by points. Nora and Zisa completely dominated their first matches and won by making their opponents tap out.

Us girls are doing it for ourselves!

This tournament was a 'Single Elimination' tournament, which meant if you lost a single match, you were out, but if you won, you would go against another person that also won. That usually meant that each match would get harder than the last match, and that was definitely true today. Although everyone won their next matches, it was obvious that the competition was getting tougher and tougher.

In the third round, Nathan lost when he got caught in a choke. Kenny barely won his match on points. Zisa and Nora won their matches and Danny and I also won ours, meaning all of us except Nathan made it to the semifinals.

Every time that Danny or I won a match, his brother Anthony was so happy. "I knew you were going to win! I knew you were going to win!" he would shout. It put a big smile on my face to see him that excited.

I'm with team Danny and Marc!

In my semifinal match, I was going against a really good kid from another school. I think he had been training longer than I had been, and he was also very strong. He got the takedown on me, and once we hit the mat, he was working really hard to pass my guard. But the harder he worked, the more tired he got. I had been running so much with Uncle Jake in addition to training jiu-jitsu that I was barely out of breath. In the last minute of the match, I felt his energy fade away, and that is when I swept him. Once I was on top, I almost immediately passed his guard, which gave me enough points to beat him.

"That's why we train hard," Uncle Jake told me after the match. He was right. I never would have won that match if I had not been in good shape from all the training and running I had done.

HOW I USED TO BE
5th grade

HOW I AM NOW
Today

Anthony was also excited that I won, giving me a hug and saying, "You are going to be the champion!"

Danny's semifinal match was also against a really good opponent, but Danny was able to score more points for the win. He was really psyched, but not as happy as Anthony, who was jumping up and down with joy.

Zisa lost her match in the semifinals, but Nora won hers. Kenny had a tough match in the semifinals and lost after getting caught in a kimura shoulder lock. He ended up with a fourth-place finish.

So in the end from our team, it was Nora, Danny, and me all fighting in the finals for first-place gold medals.

Nora went first against a really tall girl that was also really good. But she wasn't as good as Nora.

Nora trained so hard and was so focused, she seemed to make everyone else look like beginners. Every move that she made seemed a couple steps ahead of her opponent. Even in the finals, against the girl that had beat-

-en all the other girls, Nora simply connected move after move after move until she had her opponent in a triangle choke and made the girl tap out. Nora had won gold.

I was next up. My opponent looked relaxed, and because I had watched one of his earlier matches, I could tell he was skilled too.

As soon as we locked up, I could tell it was going to be a tough match. He was grabbing my gi and pushing and pulling me again and again, trying to make me lose my balance. At one point, he stuck his leg out to trip me, but I regained my balance, grabbed his leg, and took him down to the mat, where I landed inside his guard. His guard was really good—but it wasn't quite as good as Danny's guard.

He went for a choke and I defended it. He went for an armlock and I defended it.

Then he went for a kimura and I defended it, but as I did, he transitioned right into an omoplata—the same move that Danny had once done to me—and the same move Danny had shown me how to apply and how to defend.

"You know what to do!" shouted Danny from the sidelines.

He was right; I did know what to do. I grabbed my thigh near my knee to reinforce the arm he was attacking. Then I sat back for a moment and with my other hand, popped his foot over my head, and almost instantly was past his guard and across the side—with a total of four points to zero.

Once across the side, I worked hard to move to the mount, but my opponent was working hard too. In the last thirty seconds, he was able to replace his guard on me, but it was too late. Time ran out for him, and I won the match. I shook his hand and helped him up off the mat.

The referee brought us to the middle of the mat and raised my hand. It felt good to win. I walked over to the rest of my teammates who were all cheering and gave them high-fives.

When I got to Danny, I said, "Thanks."

"I didn't do anything—that was all you," he replied.

"Not true. I never would have gotten out of that omaplata if it wasn't for you."

Danny just smiled and said, "We are a team."

He was right, and just as he said that, Anthony came up with a big smile on his face and gave me a hug. "You're the champion!" he said. "You're the champion!"

The last match was Danny against a really good fighter named Tim. I had seen Tim in other jiu-jitsu tournaments, and he was one of the best around. He was totally serious about training and competing. He warmed up wearing headphones and a big robe that covered his gi to keep his muscles warm. He was like a professional and when he and Danny got on the mat, it showed.

He quickly took Danny down to the mat with a judo trip and immediately passed his guard. Once Tim passed Danny's guard, it looked like Danny could barely move. But he kept fighting.

"You've got to work from there, Danny," Coach Adam yelled from the sidelines.

After a real struggle, Danny managed to replace his guard, but it didn't last long. Tim applied some pressure, got past Danny's guard again, and then went to the mount. The score was now nine to zero for Tim.

It didn't look at all good for Danny. But he didn't give up. He kept fighting and eventually was able to elbow escape from the mount and get Tim back into his guard.

Once Tim was back inside Danny's guard, I saw it. Danny reached loosely into Tim's gi collar and grabbed it. As Tim put his head down to apply his weight and pass Danny's guard, Danny reached his other hand over Tim's head, grabbed his own sleeve and locked in the loop choke.

"You've got it!" I shouted.

It took a moment for Tim to realize what was happening. His body suddenly tensed up and he started to struggle. But it was too late. He bucked back and forth a few times, but after a few more seconds, he was done and had to tap.

"YES!" I yelled as everyone on our team jumped up in the air.

It was an incredible victory. And just like I was able to use what Danny had taught me to defend the omoplata, Danny was able to use the loop choke I had taught him to win. It felt amazing just as if I had just won another championship.

CHAPTER 21

As soon as Danny won, Anthony jumped up and yelled, "He's the champion, he's the champion!" He had a huge smile on his face. Danny and Tim got up, and the referee called them to the center of the mat where he raised Danny's hand. Danny walked off the mat, gave high fives to all of us on the team, and then got a giant hug from Anthony. It was awesome to see how thrilled Anthony was and I was glad to be friends with Anthony and Danny.

Soon an announcement came over the speaker calling us all to one side of the gymnasium to receive our awards and stand on the podium for pictures.

The podium had four platforms to stand on, the tallest one was for first place, the next tallest was for second, then third, and the shortest one was for fourth place. The winners of each weight class were called up to the podium to receive their medals. Kenny got fourth place, Zisa got third, and Nora, Danny, and I all got our first place gold medals.

It was awesome to stand on the podium and have the first place gold medal hung around my neck. I looked at Uncle Jake, and I could see he was happy I won. I stepped down from the podium and walked over to him. "Thanks, Uncle Jake."

"Don't thank me," he replied. "I didn't earn that medal. You did."

"Yes, but I couldn't have done it without you. I wouldn't even know what jiu-jitsu is if it weren't for you.

So thank you."

"I'm glad you
like jiu-jitsu. And
I'm glad you work
hard at it," he said.

I grabbed the
medal around my neck
and looked at it. GOLD. It
was still sinking in that
I had won first
place. It felt
AWESOME.

Then I walked over to Danny and gave him a high
five. "Nice work out there!" I told him.

"You too," he replied. "Thanks for teaching me that
loop choke. If I hadn't had that, there's no way I would
have beaten that kid. He was GOOD!"

"Yeah," I said. "That was AWESOME. And there is no
way I would have won if you hadn't shown me that omoplata escape! It worked like magic!"

Right then, Danny's mom, dad, and brother came over.

"Great job out there, boys," his dad said.

"Excellent work!" his mom added, giving Danny a hug.

"I knew you would be the champion!" said Anthony. "I knew it!"

Danny looked at Anthony and asked, "Do you know who the real champion is?"

"You are," Anthony replied.

"Nope," replied Danny, "you are." And with that, Danny took his medal off and put it around Anthony's neck.

"YES!" Anthony shouted as his eyes lit up, "yes! I am the champion!"

He looked at me and repeated, "I am the champion!"

I could see that medal made Anthony happier than anything else in the world. Without another thought, I said, "You're not just the champion, Anthony. You're the double champion!" as I took the medal from around my neck and put it around Anthony's.

"Really?" he asked.

"Yes! You are the double champion!"

"Double champion!" he said quietly as he looked at both medals around his neck. "Double champion," he said a little louder, and finally, at a yell, "DOUBLE CHAMPION! I AM THE DOUBLE CHAMPION!"

His smile was huge and he hugged all of us—Danny, his parents, and me. It was awesome. It felt like I had won again.

Danny smiled at me.

Mrs. Rhinehart also looked happy and gave me a hug and whispered, "Thank you," in my ear.

I looked over and saw Uncle Jake looking at me. He nodded his head.

We all said goodbye, and I walked over to Uncle Jake.

"That was a good thing to do right there, Marc."

I nodded my head in agreement.

"Should we head to the Olde Malt Shoppe and get you a double bacon cheeseburger? I think you deserve it."

"YES!" I exclaimed.

I'm expecting a healthy appetite!

We got in the car and buckled our seatbelts.

"You did good work today, Marc. Really good," Uncle Jake said after we started driving.

"Thanks, Uncle Jake."

"Let's debrief."

"Debrief?" I asked. "What's that?"

"In the SEAL Teams, after a mission, the platoon gets together to talk about what went right and what went wrong. What we could do better. What we learned. So, what did you learn today?"

"I learned a lot. I learned being in good shape can make the difference between winning and losing. I was able to wear my opponent down, and once he got tired, I was able to win. And after seeing Danny give his medal to his brother, I learned that there are more important things than winning and losing."

"Yes. Those are great lessons. And I was very impressed by both you and Danny. I know you both worked hard for those medals, and I know they meant a lot to you. For you to give that medal away—to someone that it would mean even more to—that is what a Warrior Kid does. It is called sacrifice. That was a small sacrifice, but you made Danny's brother very happy. And I hope that made you happy too."

"It did, Uncle Jake. It did," I said.

"But there is one more thing—one we already talked about, but it should be very clear right now."

"My ego?" I asked.

"That's right," Uncle Jake said. "What about it?"

"I need to control it?"

"Yes. You do. And you did. Instead of being jealous of Danny and not being his friend and avoiding training with him, you put your ego in check."

You're not making the decisions around here. I am!

"You trained with him. You got tapped out by him. Became friends with him. And those things made you better. If you hadn't put your ego in check, if you hadn't trained with him, if you hadn't put your ego aside and learned what you could from him, you never would have won today. You understand that, right?"

"Yes, I do, Uncle Jake," I replied.

"But it doesn't stop there. That is the way life is for a warrior. If you let your ego get in the way, you won't reach your potential. You won't be as good as you can be. Remember that," Uncle Jake said in a very serious tone.

"I will, Uncle Jake. I will."

We sat silently as we drove the rest of the way to the Olde Malt Shoppe. Once there, I ordered my favorite meal: a double bacon cheeseburger and a mint chocolate chip milkshake. Uncle Jake got the same thing. We joked and laughed about how good it tasted. And it did taste good.

But what was even better was knowing I had put my ego aside and become friends with Danny. I had learned from him, I had fought well in the competition and won, and, most importantly, I had made someone else's life a little bit better by giving Anthony my medal.

It was a good debrief.

CHAPTER 22

"Get up," Uncle Jake whispered in a quiet voice.

I looked at my clock and realized my alarm hadn't even gone off yet.

"But it's only–"

"No buts. Get up," Uncle Jake said firmly.

Well, there goes my beauty rest...

I started going through my mind trying to think why Uncle Jake would be mad at me. Had I done something wrong? But I couldn't think of anything. I sat up in bed, feeling sore from the jiu-jitsu tournament.

"Did I do something wrong?" I asked Uncle Jake.

"Negative," he said, "but you have something to do right."

"What?" I asked.

"Just get up, get your workout clothes on, and meet me down in the garage."

"Okay," I said. I quickly got up, got my clothes and sneakers on, and headed down to the garage.

When walked in, Uncle Jake was looking at me. "Today is the day," he said.

"What day?" I asked him.

"The day you break a six-minute mile," he replied.

More like the day a six-minute mile BREAKS YOU!

I started to tell Uncle Jake that I was still tired from the jiu-jitsu tournament, and the workouts we had been doing—and from the fact that he had woken me up earlier than usual. "But I'm—"

"But you're what?" Uncle Jake said sharply, making me want to keep my thoughts to myself. But I just didn't feel like I could do it today and I had to tell him.

"I'm sore from the jiu-jitsu tournament."

"Doesn't matter," he replied.

"And we haven't taken any rest days from working out, so my legs are sore."

"Doesn't matter," Uncle Jake repeated.

"And you woke me up earlier than usual. I just think I should get a full night's rest if I'm going to try to do this."

"Well, you aren't going to get a full night's rest. And you are going to be sore. And you are not going to try to do this. You are going to do this," Uncle Jake said in a stern voice. "Now stretch out."

I started to stretch out and get warmed up in silence.

Suddenly, Uncle Jake asked, "Do you think that conditions are always going to be perfect for you in life?"

"I guess not," I answered.

"Well, you guessed right. Things aren't always perfect. In the SEAL Teams, when we were going on a mission, things were never perfect. The weather might be bad. The gear might be broken. The terrain might be awful. The water might be too cold. The enemy might be doing something you didn't expect. But it doesn't matter. We still had to do our mission."

I listened quietly as I stretched.

"That's what we do. That's what a warrior does."

Uncle Jake was staring at me.

"It doesn't matter that you are tired. It doesn't matter that you are sore. You have a mission to do. You have trained to do it. You are capable of doing it. You are going to have to push yourself hard—but you can do this. Are you ready?"

"Yes, Uncle Jake."

"Let's go," he said.

We walked out of the garage and lined up by the driveway to start.

"Now. I am going to run the pace. You stay with me. No matter what, you stay with me. There is going to be a little voice of weakness in your head telling you to slow down, telling you that you don't have anything left, telling you to give up. Here's the thing: I want you to tell that little voice to BE QUIET with something called WILL. Do you know what will is Marc?" Uncle Jake asked.

"I'm not sure, Uncle Jake."

"Will is determination. It is resolve. Will is when you hear that little voice and you feel like you are going to break, but instead of listening to that little voice you dig deep and KEEP GOING. Understand? That's will. You KEEP GOING."

"Yes, Uncle Jake," I told him. I still wasn't sure I could keep pace with Uncle Jake, but I was sure going to try.

"Okay," Uncle Jake said. "Here we go...standby...BUST 'EM!"

With that, Uncle Jake sprinted off. I stayed with him. He was going at a fast pace, but I ran hard and stayed close.

After the first block, I was feeling pretty good. But that didn't last long. I started breathing harder. My legs started to feel tired.

"Dig deep," Uncle Jake said. "KEEP GOING."

I didn't respond because I was breathing too hard. But I was staying with him.

I stayed right next to him for a while, but as we got to the corner, I started to fade a little bit behind him.

"STAY WITH ME! KEEP GOING!" he shouted.

It shocked me a little to hear Uncle Jake shout and I reflexively stepped out and caught up with him.

As we approached the corner to head up the hill, Uncle Jake said, "Alright, we are going to attack this hill. Get ready."

I didn't respond. I just kept running as hard as I could. When we turned the corner and started up the hill, Uncle Jake attacked and picked up the pace even more.

I felt like I was going to run out of energy. There was no way I was going to be able to keep up this pace. I could hear that little voice in my head saying that I needed to slow down to ease the strain on my legs and my lungs. I heard that little voice saying I didn't have anything left. But I told that little voice to be quiet and said to myself, *keep going. Just a little farther. KEEP GOING.*

As we ran up the hill, I thought I was going to collapse, but I just kept going.

When we finally got to the top of the hill and tagged the fence, I felt like I was going to die. I thought to myself, *well, I have tried hard, but I just don't have anything left.*

"HALFWAY!" Uncle Jake yelled. "KEEP GOING!"

So I did. I took a big step, then another, then another.

Just...
keep...
going...

As we approached the bottom of the hill at the corner, I thought the hard part of the run was over. But it wasn't. The hill had drained me, and I felt like I needed to back off just a little bit.

But Uncle Jake didn't back off at all.

"KEEP GOING!" he barked. "COME ON!"

So I stepped it up again.

Then I realized something. Every time I thought I was done—every time I heard that little voice telling me to slow down, every time I thought I had nothing left, I was able to find my WILL and KEEP GOING.

And that is what I did. I KEPT GOING. I ignored my tired legs, I ignored the pain in my lungs and KEPT GOING.

Finally, I could see my driveway—the finish line.

"Almost there," Uncle Jake said. "Almost there. Finish strong!"

Now I was through the pain. The nagging little voice of weakness in my head was silent. I pushed as hard as I could—as hard as I had ever pushed myself in my life. Uncle Jake and I were in an all out sprint as we came across the finish line.

I took a few more steps, collapsed onto the driveway, shut my eyes, and took some giant breaths as I tried to settle down.

"Hey," I heard Uncle Jake say. I opened my eyes and he was standing over me. "Five-fifty-three. You did it."

"AAAhhhhh," I groaned. Although I tried to say, "YES!" it didn't quite come out that way. But it didn't matter—Uncle Jake knew what I meant.

"Good work, Marc. That's how you push yourself."

"MMMmmmm," I replied—trying to say thanks, but not being able to put the words together. Uncle Jake laughed.

After a few minutes, I got my breath back, stood up and gave Uncle Jake a high five.

"That's what I'm talking about. You didn't listen to that little voice of weakness. You used your will and you kept going."

"I did, Uncle Jake."

Uncle Jake stood there quietly for a few seconds before he said, "This isn't just about running you know, right?"

I gave him a puzzled look, because I didn't know what he meant.

"Marc, this is about life. This is about facing challenges. *This is about everything.*"

This is about everything.

"Remember how hard you worked a few summers ago to be able to do ten pull-ups?" Uncle Jake asked.

"Of course I do," I replied.

"You couldn't do any pull-ups when the summer started, but we made a plan, and you worked hard, and you made it happen. And like I told you, you can do that with almost anything in life. Well, it's the same thing here. You can always push yourself a little bit harder. If your will is strong, you can always dig a little deeper. Where there is a will, there is a way. Even if you can only move another foot—or another inch—you can always keep going. That's your will, Marc. WILL. And if you have a strong will and apply that determination to everything you do, you will be able to accomplish almost any goal you can set for yourself. And the more you build your will by doing hard things, the stronger your will becomes. If you have a strong will—almost nothing can stop you."

"Will is a powerful thing, Marc. A very powerful thing. Remember that, Marc. Always remember that," Uncle Jake said.

I will, Uncle Jake," I said.

As we walked up to the house, the sun wasn't even up yet.

And I felt something. A new feeling. I felt more confident and stronger than I had ever felt before. I felt like I could overcome any challenge if I worked hard and set my mind to it.

I felt the power of my will.

And it felt good.

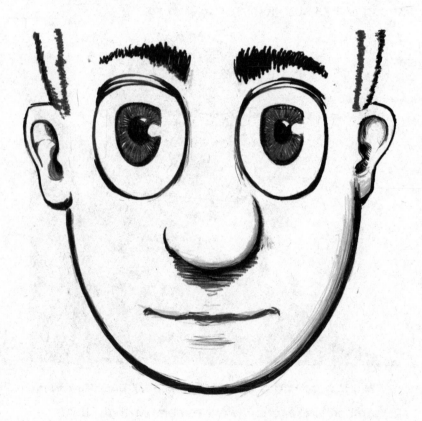

CHAPTER 23

A few days later, when I walked downstairs to go work out, I saw Uncle Jake's bag packed up, sitting by the door. That is when it hit me: the summer was almost over and Uncle Jake was heading back to college.

I went out to the garage, and Uncle Jake was already there.

"Last workout with me for the summer," he said with a smile.

"I can't believe it is over already. Summer always goes by so fast."

"Yes, it does. And life does the same thing," Uncle Jake said quietly.

I wasn't sure what he meant by that, so I asked, "What?"

"You'll see, Marc. Life goes by quickly—like a summer day. It never seems that way when you are young, but when you get a little older, you'll see. Life goes by fast. So don't waste any time. You don't get a second chance." Uncle Jake stood for a minute looking at me with a serious face. Then he gave me a little smile and said, "Speaking of wasting time. Let's stop wasting time and get this workout done!"

We did a hundred pull-ups, a hundred push-ups, a hundred sit-ups, and a hundred squats. Then we went outside and ran a mile—but not too hard.

"You can't push yourself to the maximum every day, Marc. You will over train and wear yourself out. Your performance will go down. So, you have to make sure you back off sometimes and let your body and mind recover. Okay?"

"Yes, Uncle Jake."

"But that doesn't mean sit around and do nothing—that's not good either. Still move and stretch and do something everyday to keep yourself on track. To maintain the discipline. Understand?"

"I sure do, Uncle Jake," I told him. "Discipline equals freedom."

"It sure does."

DISCIPLINE EQUALS FREEDOM

After we finished our run and ate a quick breakfast, it was time to take Uncle Jake to the airport.

My mom drove us to the airport, and we didn't say much on the car ride there. But my mom did ask Uncle Jake what he was going to do when he finished college.

Uncle Jake explained that he was going to go back into the SEAL Teams, but this time as an officer, which meant he would be in more of a leadership position.

Of course, I was a little sad when we got to the airport, but it was okay. I knew Uncle Jake and I would talk on the phone and I would see him during Thanksgiving and Christmas breaks.

Uncle Jake got out of the car, and my mom and I got out to say goodbye.

"We'll see you in a few months, Jake," my mom said as she gave him a hug.

"Yes, you will," he replied with a smile on his face, "and thanks for everything."

"Thanks to you too," she said as she looked over at me and nodded her head.

Uncle Jake held out his hand, and I gave him a good, hard handshake.

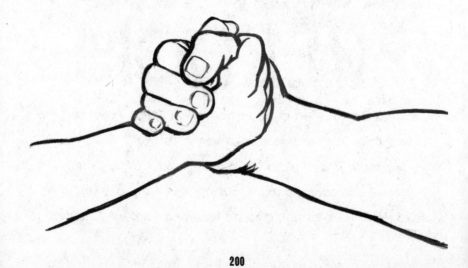

"Okay, Marc. I'll see you when I see you," he said with a smile. But then he got serious and said, "You're doing good things right now. Remember to keep your ego in check. Don't judge people. Keep digging deep, pushing yourself, and using the power of your will to keep going. Most of all, stay on The Path of being a Warrior Kid, okay?"

"I will, Uncle Jake," I told him.

He picked up his bag and walked away.

My mom and I got back into the car and headed home.

"It's always sad to see him go," my mom said.

"He'll be back," I told her.

"Yes, he will," she replied and smiled a quiet smile.

When we got home I walked up to my room and looked at my Warrior Kid code.

1. The Warrior Kid wakes up early in the morning.
2. The Warrior Kid studies to learn and gain knowledge and asks questions if they don't understand.
3. The Warrior Kid trains hard, exercises, and eats right to be strong and fast and healthy.
4. The Warrior Kid trains to know how to fight so they can stand up to bullies and protect the weak.
5. The Warrior Kid treats people with respect and helps out other people whenever possible.
6. The Warrior Kid keeps things neat and is always prepared and ready for action.
7. The Warrior Kid stays humble and stays calm. Warrior Kids do not lose their tempers.
8. The Warrior Kid works hard, saves money, is frugal and doesn't waste things, and always does their best.
9. I am the Warrior Kid and I am a leader.

I thought about how I had judged Danny when I first met him. He made me mad because he didn't want to come over my house. I didn't know that he had to take care of his brother Anthony. I judged him without knowing him. I had done the same thing last year with Nathan. I judged him as sloppy because his clothes were a mess. I didn't know that his family didn't have money for nice clothes. I needed to remember not to judge people. So I took my pen and changed number five of my Warrior Kid code to read:

5. The Warrior Kid treats people with respect, doesn't judge them, and helps out other people whenever possible.

Then I thought about what Uncle Jake had taught me about my ego. I had let my ego get out of control with Danny. That was not good. I needed to remember that. I took my pen out and changed number seven of my Warrior Kid code to read:

7. The Warrior Kid stays humble, controls their ego, and stays calm. Warrior Kids do not lose their tempers.

When I was done, I decided to write a letter to Uncle Jake and send him my new Warrior Kid Code. This is what I wrote him:

Dear Uncle Jake,

Thank you for coming to stay with us this summer and thank you for what you taught me while you were here. You taught me to keep my ego under control so my ego doesn't control me. You also taught me to make sure I don't judge people. I should have learned that lesson from Nathan James, but I didn't, and I still judged Danny Rhinehart the same way, without understanding what was going on in his life.

This summer you also taught me to use my will and that I can push myself even harder than I ever thought possible. Now I know that when things are tough or I feel like I don't have anything left, I can use my will to dig deep and KEEP GOING!

I know these things are very important, so I added them to my Warrior Kid Code.

Here is my newest Warrior Kid code:

1. The Warrior Kid wakes up early in the morning.
2. The Warrior Kid studies to learn and gain knowledge and asks questions if they don't understand.
3. The Warrior Kid trains hard, exercises, and eats right to be strong and fast and healthy.
4. The Warrior Kid trains to know how to fight so they can stand up to bullies and protect the weak.
5. The Warrior Kid treats people with respect, doesn't judge them, and helps out other people whenever possible.
6. The Warrior Kid keeps things neat and is always prepared and ready for action.
7. The Warrior Kid stays humble, controls their ego, and stays calm. Warrior Kids do not lose their tempers.
8. The Warrior Kid works hard, saves money, is frugal, and doesn't waste things, and always does their best.
9. I am the Warrior Kid and I am a leader.

Thanks for everything, Uncle Jake.
I will stay on The Path of being a Warrior Kid.

Marc

I folded up the letter, put it in an envelope with a stamp and brought it outside to the mailbox at the end of the driveway.

After I put the letter in the mailbox, I looked down the street where I had run all summer. It seemed like only yesterday that summer had started, and now it was gone.

I thought about what Uncle Jake said about life going by fast, just like summer days. I guess that was what he was talking about.

"Don't waste it," I heard Uncle Jake say in my head.

I won't, I thought to myself.

I jogged back to the house, went to my room and started to get my things for school out. School was starting in a couple days and I wanted to be ready—ready for school and ready for life. Time goes by quickly and I didn't want to waste it.

Then I thought about everything I had learned from Uncle Jake and I realized that every time I think I know a lot, he teaches me something new, every time I felt like I was getting to the end of The Path, there is a little bit farther to go.

And I'm not sure if I will ever reach the end of The Path.

But I do know this: I am going to stay on it.

Turn the page for a look at the first book
in the Way of the Warrior Kid series!

CHAPTER 1: THE WORST YEAR

Tomorrow is the last day of school, and I CAN'T WAIT FOR IT TO BE OVER!! This has been the worst year EVER! The bad part is that I don't see how next year is going to be any better at all. Fifth grade was horrible—I'm afraid sixth grade will be EVEN WORSE. Why was it so bad? Where do I begin?

This is ME (Marc).

I'm the hot dog-eating champ in my house!

This guy can beat me in a foot race.

Top five reasons why fifth grade was HORRIBLE:

1. It's school! I'm sitting at a desk ALL DAY.
2. I learned that I'm dumb! That's right. All the other grades I thought I was "smart." But this year was a FAILURE! I still don't know my times tables! How the heck am I going to make it through next year?

0x0=

3. School lunches. They call it "pizza." I have no idea why. Since when does a piece of white bread count as pizza crust???????

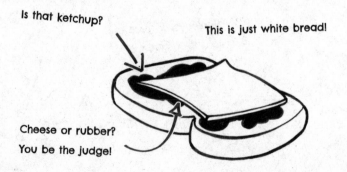

Is that ketchup?

This is just white bread!

Cheese or rubber? You be the judge!

4. Gym class. Most people like gym. But at my school we have "tests" and I completely stink. Especially at PULL-UPS. Guess how many pull-ups I can do? ZERO! I can do ZERO pull-ups! I'm a disgrace to ten-year-olds—and the whole class knows it. Even the girls. Especially the girls that can do more pull-ups than me!!

5. Field trips. Just like gym class, most kids like field trips. Well, we go to one place for field trips: Mount Tom. We go there in the fall before it gets too cold and in the spring when it starts to get warm. But here's the thing: Mount Tom isn't a mountain. It's a lake. Here's the problem: I CAN'T SWIM! I hid it pretty well during our fall trip. But this spring,

kids noticed. "Why don't you come out in the water?" "Why are you staying on the beach?" "Why don't you jump off the diving board?" What kind of person can't even swim? ME: That's what kind of person! AAAHHH!

6. I know I said top five reasons, but there is one more, and it's probably the biggest reason: Kenny Williamson. He is big and he is MEAN. He rules the jungle gym. He even calls himself "King of the Jungle Gym" or "King Kenny"!! If any other kids want to play on the jungle gym, they either have to be friends with Kenny or follow his "rules."

These things could hurt someone!

A HUMAN TIME BOMB!

All the teachers talk about how my school is "bully-free." We even had a No Bully Day, where we talked about bullying and how bad it was and how we should tell the teachers if we saw it happening. Well, let me tell you, Kenny is definitely a BULLY, and he definitely is in my school. And no one says anything to the teachers about it!

Those are the top reasons that fifth grade was horrible, and sixth grade isn't going to be much better! I can't wait for school to be over tomorrow so the suffering can STOP and summer can START!

This summer is going to be AWESOME. Yes, it is cool that I won't have to be in school—but something even cooler is happening. My uncle Jake is coming to stay with us for the whole summer!

He has been a Navy SEAL for eight years and is getting out of the Navy to go to college. Before he goes to college, he is going to stay with us the whole summer long. A Navy SEAL! FOR REAL. IN MY HOUSE!!!!!

Uncle Jake is the best. First, he is super cool because he is a Navy SEAL. He fought in real wars. My mom says he was "on the front lines." That means he was face-to-face with the bad guys. Whoa! Uncle Jake is also awesome because he is the COMPLETE OPPOSITE OF ME. I am weak—he is strong. I am dumb—he is smart. I can't swim—he can swim with a backpack on! I'm scared of bullies—bullies are scared of him!

MY UNCLE JAKE!!

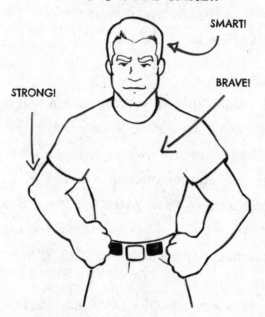

SMART!

BRAVE!

STRONG!

Anyway, I haven't spent too much time with Uncle Jake because we live in California, and he has been stationed in Virginia for a long time. I hope he doesn't think I'm such a DUMB WIMP that he won't even hang around with me! Maybe he won't notice?

AAHHHHH!!! Of course he will. He is a tough guy! I'm a dork! Well, I guess I will find out soon.